...le Say Goodbye can do infinitely more for
...e between the two people than hundreds
...al goodwill talks I have heard."

**...shid, former head of the Palestinian
...tion in Italy**

...e We Say Goodbye gives us a rare look and a
...erful opportunity to get to know reality from
...ird's-eye view, with all its complexity and
m... faces. It does not embellish it. It does not
b... ...e or judge, nor does it get tangled in political
a... ...sations of who is better off or who is hurting
... ...e. It mourns, it despairs and it hurts, but it is
... ...tally honest. And that is where its importance
...es. That is where its magic lies."

**Vered Cohen-Barzilay, Director of
Communications and Publications,
Amnesty International Israel**

BEFORE WE SAY GOODBYE

GABRIELLA AMBROSIO

Translated by Alastair McEwen

**WALKER
BOOKS**

First published in Great Britain 2010 by Walker Books Ltd
87 Vauxhall Walk, London SE11 5HJ

2 4 6 8 10 9 7 5 3 1

Original edition: *Prima di Lasciarsi* © 2004 Gabriella Ambrosio
English translation © 2010 Alastair McEwen
Cover image © 2010 Luis Costa / Photolibrary.com

This book has been typeset in Fairfield

Printed and bound in Great Britain by Clays Ltd, St Ives plc

British Library Cataloguing in Publication Data:
a catalogue record for this book is available from the British Library

ISBN 978-1-4063-2504-1

www.walker.co.uk

Inspired by the true story of
Ayat al-Akhras and Rachel Levy

MAIN CHARACTERS:

Abdelin, 38, Dima's aunt and her fiancé's mother; Palestinian

Abraham, 59, a security guard; an Israeli Jew who was breast-fed by an Arab woman

Adum a haulage contractor; Palestinian

Dima, 18, top of her class at school; Palestinian

Faris, 20, Dima's cousin and fiancé, a tiler; Palestinian

Ghassan, 23, an unemployed Palestinian; an explosives expert

Leila Oder a star journalist with Arab television station al-Arabiya

Lia, 37, Abraham's wife

Marwad and *Safiya* and their sons, *Khaldun* and *Ibrahim*, live across the way from Dima; Palestinian

Michael, 18, Myriam's "American" friend; Israeli

Myriam, 18, spends some time at school and some time on the hill; an Israeli Jewess

Nathan, 19, Myriam's brother, doing his military service at the Erez checkpoint; an Israeli Jew

Rizak, 25, Ghassan's acquaintance and owner of an old red van; Palestinian

Said, 54, Dima's father, a foreman with an Israeli construction company; Palestinian

Sara, 61, a clerk with the company that employs Abraham; an Israeli Jewess

Shoshi, 45, Myriam and Nathan's mother; an Israeli Jewess

Vered, 50, a pacifist and Shoshi's friend; an Israeli Jewess

EXTRAS:

Israeli workers at the site where Said works
Inhabitants of Dheisheh, a Palestinian refugee camp
Soldiers from the Israeli army
Workers in the mortuary

JERUSALEM, 29 MARCH 2002

7 A.M.

DIMA DOESN'T LISTEN TO LEILA AND GOES OUT

It was technically springtime on the day that Dima got up from her mattress after a long yet strangely brief and confused night. She switched on the television as she did on any other day, and the journalist Leila Oder appeared before her as she did on any other day. Leila was giving a news item which Dima didn't understand. So she lit the gas ring, and since it wasn't just any other day, the smell of the gas slipped straight into her veins and began to flow slowly through her blood.

Leila Oder didn't take her eyes off Dima that morning as she spoke to her from the al-Arabiya news desk. Now *she* was the spectator, watching Dima drinking her coffee, which slid down slowly, ever so slowly, and blended with the blood and the gas inside her.

Everything would be slow that morning, slow and dull to avoid getting hurt. Even Dima's smile was slow and dull as she turned back from the door to embrace everything and everyone in one glance, as if to photograph them, and to remain photographed there herself, all in one piece – head, arms and feet. Feet that did not move from there, yet they eventually did and finally carried her out.

It had rained throughout the night and the street was a sea of mud all the way to school. Dima's shoes became heavier and heavier, sinking into the mud, and she didn't think about Leila. She trudged through the mud with her mouth wide open. And that's how she was when she came across Jihan, who would later say, "Her expression wasn't that of someone who wants to talk. So we said hello and I went on my way."

MYRIAM IS IN THE COMPANY OF MICHAEL

At that same moment, Myriam found herself with Michael. They were on the hill of Tiberias, breathing deeply; the air slipped under their skin as the sun traced squares on the fruit trees. They were shouting into the distance, no one could hear them, when the alarm clock rang. She would have switched it off and carried on dreaming, had it not been the day of her school photography exhibition.

All the trees of Jerusalem were waiting for her, lined up in rows behind glass panes, hanging from the walls of the school corridors. Olive trees, fig trees, grapevines, pines, acacias, convolvuluses; full suns on the horizon, gnarled boughs and strong boughs. Perhaps this was why she had dreamed that Michael was shouting with her up on a hill. This morning her trees at the school were forming an avenue along the corridor all the way down to Michael's corner. She closed her eyes again and imagined that the last few trees bowed towards Michael's photo.

She smiled at the thought, and found the strength to get out of bed. She went into the bathroom, where she looked in the mirror and reminded herself that Michael was dead.

"Sooner or later you'll have to come to terms with it," said her mother when she saw Myriam come into the kitchen with a lost look.

"I'm gonna," said Myriam in her funny English, taking her jacket and going out.

Her mother was left alone.

ABRAHAM GETS UP

In another house the phone rang at seven, while Abraham and Lia were still in bed, his arm round her shoulder, one of her long legs over his back.

"Did I wake you, Abraham?" laughed old Sara on the other end of the line.

"You know it's always a pleasure to hear from you, Sara," replied Abraham as he stifled a yawn.

"They're asking for two replacements today," said Sara, "one for the Artists' Restaurant and one for the supermarket in Kiryat Yovel."

"If I can choose, I'll go for the supermarket," he said. "I don't feel like working late tonight."

"Of course, Abraham, that's precisely why I called you. Only you'll have to hurry – the supermarket opens at eight."

"I'm already up," he replied, sitting on the edge of the bed and feeling for his slippers with swollen feet.

Lia heaved herself up from the other side with a yawn, grabbed her dressing gown and headed for the bathroom. "I can see you're in a rush; I'll make you some coffee," she promised, tidying her hair with her hands before closing the door behind her.

GHASSAN IS ALREADY ON THE ROAD

Ghassan had got up before everyone that morning, and it was still raining when he went out. His one brown eye and one blue eye glittered beneath the tiny droplets on his lashes. In the rain he walked unseen to Rizak's house, where Rizak gave him a small heavy bag and the keys to the van. Ghassan stowed the bag under the seat, switched on the engine, put the van in gear. As he adjusted the mirror he first turned it towards him and took a good look at himself. The water was running down his black curls onto his face, which broke into a smile. His heart leaped with a deep satisfaction.

He looked towards the distant city, which still seemed asleep. "Wait a few hours and you'll get your wake-up call," he murmured. He looked at the sky and thought that the fine weather was returning.

Ghassan was twenty-three, and today he felt strong. His only fear was that he might suddenly get one of his terrible migraines. He pressed on the accelerator, and with head held high he drove the van home. A faint smile danced at the corners of his handsome mouth. When he got back, he hid the van as best he could behind the house and took the bag with him. It had stopped raining, and in the distance, in the direction of Jerusalem, the sky was brightening.

Everything seemed under Ghassan's control that morning, even the sun as it broke through the clouds and urged everyone out of their homes to meet their fate.

ON THE STREET DIMA THINKS ABOUT A WINDOW ACROSS THE WAY

Meanwhile, Dima continued to make her way through the mud, staring fixedly ahead.

A window into a room across the street had been the

17

only proof, in the long days of the recent curfew, that the world was still going on. Marwad and Safiya and their children, who were growing up in that room. There was nothing else to do but grow, in those circumstances. And there was nothing else Dima could do but watch them. The street that separated their houses was only a few arm spans wide, and the old broken windows of the Dheisheh refugee camp were not windows with curtains.

On the first day of the curfew little Ibrahim had begun to crawl on all fours. On the fifteenth he took three steps at a run, throwing himself from his mother's arms into his father's. By the twentieth he was moving about with the aid of the sofa. That day he got hold of a piece of soap and with it he rubbed Khaldun, who was ten months older than he was and had the patience of an old man. Together they would fall down and get up, lean against each other and tug each other, pointing to new horizons every time. The world was theirs, the three by two metres of that room. What lay beyond, they would see sooner or later. But there was no hurry. Their voices filled Dima's long days without an outside or an event, without light, without time.

Faris could not reach her from Bethlehem because of the curfew. Their wedding plans, as the exhausted hours gradually dripped from the days, seemed further and further away: perhaps illegitimate. Faris's evening visit was another right that had been eliminated. Another punishment on the way. And there was nothing to do.

There was
nothing
to do.

Leila Oder hadn't come to see Dima any more either. While broadcasting the unrest live from the streets, she had been wounded by a rubber bullet and had vanished from the screen, to be replaced by other reporters. But no one was as good as she was at giving the world the news from Palestine. And no one was as capable as she was of looking Dima straight in the eye as she spoke.

Without Faris, without Leila, without school; in a paralysis of action and a deterioration of thought. The window across the street had taken Dima far away. Where there was no difference between yesterday today and tomorrow, where the past was a hole, the present didn't exist and the future was the same; where there were two children who were strong, who were learning, who were growing and who were laughing.

But one day the window had suddenly shut. And everything had begun urgently and unstoppably demanding to settle accounts.

So that morning, Dima stared fixedly ahead, and in front of her now she saw nothing more than a wall. For a moment, she hoped the earth would open up to swallow her and all the walls. Instead she went into school with eyes lowered and headed straight for her desk.

To get back to Myriam. It's important to know this about her: her trees didn't stop breathing once they were in a photo. On looking carefully, you could see that they didn't even stop growing. Now some had gone beyond the frame, branches suddenly intoxicated by spring.

That was what did not disappoint her about this land: the trees. A miracle among the many – too many – stones and the thick dust and the gusty breath of the desert. A miracle, the trees planted there, growing sturdier by the day. And so Myriam had begun to photograph trees. Framed in a viewfinder, things immediately seemed clearer. A tree was a tree, claiming the right to exist, to remain planted there, peacefully reaching up towards the sky.

It had been a stroke of luck for her the day someone at school had thought of organizing a photography competition. That way, she'd had a pretext to leave school every day and go off alone up onto the hill, which was the only thing she felt like doing at that time. And she had found so much material, unexpectedly even fuller, stronger and more solid in the finished images than when she actually took the shots.

When she had handed in her photos the week before, she had peeked at the other students' entries, and none of them had struck her as up to much – except Ella's. She had photographed all kinds of water: fountains, puddles, rain, gutters, jets. Myriam had liked those almost as much as her trees.

In any event, Myriam was sure she would do well today. But as she was about to pass through the main school gate, she realized that she was no longer interested in the exhibition at all. So, instead of going into school, she turned once more in the direction of the hill.

She caught a bus. Her mother had said I beg you, please don't ever do that; but it didn't matter, she was fine; she was part of a living, breathing nature.

ABRAHAM DAYDREAMS AS HE DODGES THE PUDDLES

By now Abraham was on the road too, but still not entirely awake. This morning he wished for a gentler sun that would carry him away. Plump swarthy arms that would cradle him. A lullaby, an ancient lament. Walking quickly among the puddles towards the supermarket, he sensed those odours those flavours that accent all of which fell upon him at once, and as usual when he least expected it. Like a wave, like an echo. Like a melody. This morning. Arab eyes watching him. They were all around him. He could sense their warm pulsing. A deep pulsing, a dark breathing, a zone of shadow. Inside him. Somewhere they were waiting for him. They were calling him. They were hot on his heels.

Abraham wanted to surrender to it. Slow his pace. He

wanted to return their look, which made him feel warm and uneasy. But he didn't know how; he had forgotten.

Taking care to leap over a particularly large puddle, he shook off the feeling and laughed. It was no time, he said to himself, for daydreaming. In the days leading up to Pesach the supermarkets were particularly crowded, and that was precisely why they had called him in. To lend an extra hand, to check out every Arab who came close.

He arrived at the supermarket and went to his station. His was a backup post, just inside the entrance doors. Which were about to open.

8 A.M.

MYRIAM THINKS ABOUT A TATTOOED ARM

Had she seen the arm, perhaps she would have come to terms with it sooner. They had shown it to Michael's father for identification; it was all that remained of him but it was enough, because it was his tattooed left arm. Four of them had accompanied him to have the tattoo done. Michael had chosen a winged dragon, and one day that winged dragon had flown into the sky and then landed intact, whereas Michael had gone goodness knows where and never returned.

When they killed her mother's cousin, the one who had made a home in the territories, and even her father had come back to stay with the family for the occasion, death had not shot her inside in this way. Everyone around her had despaired and recalled and inveighed against the tribulations of their people. Her mother had wept, as had her cousin's wife, and the children, and Myriam too had cried at the funeral, until the last shovelful of earth had put an end to the matter for her. And that was normal. Because everyone has deaths in the family, especially when you go to live among the Arabs, where they don't want you and you stay there precisely because you don't want them.

But on the day they buried the Michael arm, her stomach was flattened against her belly and her head was four thousand metres up, with a void of panic in the middle; and disconnected like this she had not wept. It was as if the Michael remains were somewhere, and would arrive and put the other arm around her shoulder.

The funeral had not put an end to the matter.

Michael had been the first friend she had made when her family returned from California. He was her American friend, who like her didn't even entertain the thought of speaking Hebrew at home. She and Michael had spent most of their free time together, and had been together that day in the shopping centre, talking nineteen to the dozen in the American slang they remembered less and less – mixed when necessary with some funny or indomitable Hebrew word – and they had gone their separate ways maybe ten minutes before the explosion. Then Michael had vanished, and with him every illusion about America.

All this had happened two months before. It was

since then, since they had buried Michael's arm, that Myriam had begun to photograph trees. The still air of the hill was the only thing that calmed her. Among the trunks and the greenery she found her place again. She felt good there.

Michael was there too. He was there somewhere. She didn't know where, but she felt he was there.

DIMA HAS A SPECIAL APPOINTMENT

"You are ready. From now on you mustn't think about anything," Ghassan had told her the previous day.

But how could she not think about anything? Dima tried, with her notebook in front of her and her pen in her hand. She stared at the page without seeing it and tried not to see anything at all. Then she saw Leila smiling at her from the al-Arabiya news desk. And a hand seized her heart and clutched it tight, until it almost broke. She closed her eyes and breathed very slowly to reopen her heart. She tried her best not to let herself be hurt.

In the days of the curfew Leila had stopped coming to see her, and little by little Dima had got out of the habit of asking her advice. Yet there had been times when Leila's had been the most important voice to speak to her in those four rooms, in those fifty square metres in which thirteen of them grew up and aged. Four small connecting rooms in which there alternated all the voices of the world: the soft tender tones of the women, her father's solemn tones, her brothers' heated tones, the cheerful tones of her sisters-in-law and the sweet voices of the youngest children. And in which, at seven in the morning and three in the afternoon, every day, she heard only Leila's voice. There was rioting in Gaza; the settlers had shot at two boys. A house had been blown up by the soldiers and the occupants hadn't even had time to save their children's school certificates. An old man had been arrested but it wasn't yet known what he was accused of; his wife declared that it was impossible to find out any information about him.

Leila went into homes; the camera followed, recounted, denounced. Leila went where Dima could not go, not yet. Leila spoke loud and clear. It was all so obvious when Leila spoke. In this way she made injustice and brutality public. The future would be dead if someone didn't shake it like this, give it no respite, make sure it didn't stop.

That's why today Dima had a date with the future, in her own way, somewhere. A question of hours.

She struggled to focus on the task before her.

SHOSHI SITS AND THINKS ABOUT HER CHILDREN

Myriam's mother called the office to say she wasn't feeling well, but maybe she would go in later. And after putting down the receiver she remained seated on the chair next to the phone.

She hadn't even managed to tell her daughter, before Myriam left the house, what a terrible night she had passed. On the other hand she had asked her, the evening before, if she would mind sleeping in her bed with her, but Myriam had refused – and not very kindly either. So Shoshi had spent the entire night struggling with her breathing. Enduring the mocking tricks her mind had played on her. Trying to imagine Nathan sleeping in the barracks like a baby and not on guard, an armed man in the night. My God, Nathan *was* a child; he was only nineteen. But this land asked for your children before you had time to explain anything to them.

Nathan was doing his military service at the Erez checkpoint. He had gone off with a clear gaze, and on his first leave had returned moody and silent. Everyone knew what had happened. A Palestinian boy had blown himself up when they had been about to search him; and with him had blown up Moshe, Ariel, Samuel and Abigail. Ariel and Abigail had been Nathan's schoolmates; Ariel had been his friend since his first class in Israel. The madcap, cheeky one. The one who always loved to shock.

No one had asked Nathan any questions; everyone expected him to talk about it; everyone expected to weep with him. But he did not say what had happened. He didn't even say anything to Ariel's parents when he went to visit them. Now Nathan always had a shadow over his eyes. He no longer looked anyone in the eyes. Yet he had always been the enthusiastic one, the one who wanted to understand, the one ready to ask and to give. At nineteen, at a time when all the strengths of a boy should begin to bear fruit and new seeds, where had Nathan ended up?

Not Myriam; Myriam had always been different. Myriam never showed much interest in what others around her said or did. When had Shoshi ever managed to get her to listen to something of the spiderweb of arguments that every day she doggedly tried to spin between her children and the reality of events. Spiderwebs that in truth she desperately needed to spin for herself even more than for the children. Myriam was the one who simply switched off the television when it reported news of attacks. She was the one who simply switched off when her mother begged her not to take the bus, not to frequent closed and crowded places. She was the one who always pretended she lived in a normal country.

But after Nathan returned to Erez, Michael was blown up. From that moment, Myriam had definitively disappeared – to where, no one knew. Shoshi should have tried to talk to her, but Myriam had never let her before, and perhaps she thought she already understood everything now. Beneath a barely ruffled surface, Myriam was evidently working on discarding all that she knew and re-establishing order within herself, in her own way.

As the telephone rang, Shoshi suddenly felt an intense cold.

9 A.M.

DIMA SMILES WITHOUT MEANING TO

Dima told herself it was time to solve the equation in front of her. She'd never had any problems with maths. If she managed to clear her mind, if she managed to keep her pain in a corner, if she managed to control her panting breath: in short, if she managed to solve the equation, she would show she was ready. Without having to worry about anything any more. As Ghassan had said.

About nothing.

Nothingness.

Nothing.

Her dreams had been nothing, come to think of it now. Her successes had been nothing. Her world nothing. Her efforts nothing, her thoughts nothing. Those long hours spent with Leila: nothing.

For no one could know, but every time the news ended, Leila stayed on to talk to Dima.

Sometimes Dima would find Leila sitting opposite her on a cushion, and it didn't matter if little Nejma was playing on it. Or she would appear beside her as she toasted chickpeas. And so they would carry on talking about current events, and about what could happen. Of Dima's everyday life, and how it had been influenced by the beating of a butterfly's wings in Texas. Leila was understanding things, orientation, the conquest of the world, anger and remedy. Leila was her sister, her confidante, her friend. Leila was her role model. And Dima would have followed her.

Abu Said, her father, agreed. As he would say later, "I have always tried to give my children what I never had; I was glad she wanted to study. She wanted to do something useful, something important. So I gave her my permission, and she would have succeeded. She was always top of her class."

In the autumn, with her diploma awarded, and married to Faris, Dima would enrol for the journalism course in Bethlehem. Many times had she diverted from her usual route to pass by the college. It was a new building, still unscathed by the fury of the clashes. From the pavement opposite, Dima would observe teachers and students coming out of lessons together, always fervently absorbed in conversation.

Luckily not even Faris had opposed this plan. He had always liked her determination. Anything Dima suggested would have made him happy – he had known that since they were children. It was Dima, for example, who had chosen the games when they were small, but none of the boys in the family had ever found this strange; she knew what she was doing. She was the one who decided: we'll be the Palestinians; you'll be the Israeli soldiers. Because that was the game they played all the time on the streets of the camp, some of them arming themselves with branches wrapped in old rags as if they were rifles, while the others had stones. But Dima never played the Israeli soldier who browbeats the Palestinian. She fled into hiding, lay in wait, pretended to throw her stone, yelled, small furrows of anger running across her little forehead, but it always ended with her and her people being arrested and knocked about – in pretence – and forced to stand pressed up against the wall to be threatened and mocked.

The school of journalism was not even opposed by Faris's mother, Abdelin, in whose house Dima would go to live after the wedding, and with whom she would share the task of looking after the family. Abdelin was Dima's aunt, who had lived with their family in Dheisheh before marrying. She had never had any girls, and she had loved her niece since the day she was born.

What will Abdelin think about what will happen today? Dima almost smiled. She imagined her aunt's expression, the cries she would let out, and she felt a little consoled.

The thought of Aunt Abdelin brought back fond memories. Of when she was small, when Abdelin would sometimes come to call and play at *beit biut* with her: make up her face and lend her her high-heeled shoes, and call her "madam" and pay her visits with great ceremony, as Dima pretended to offer her coffee with cardamom. Or of the day Abdelin had taught Faris and her to play at seven stones, and of all the subsequent evenings she had spent this way, on the floor in the corner where her mother cooked on the Primus stove, showing off in front of Suad and Guivara, who were too small to be able to toss a pebble in the air and catch it while picking up the others, and so gazed at her with great envy.

Or of when – and she was bigger then – her aunt had taught her to play draughts, which was Abdelin's favourite game; and to this day, when she could, her aunt still challenged her to games and return games. The question of who was the better of the two would never be resolved.

Dima realized that her heart was warming, so she hastened to tear up all thoughts of Abdelin, just as you tear up pages that are no longer of any use.

SHOSHI SPEAKS ON THE PHONE

"No, I'm not coming, and you won't persuade me this time."

"Look, I just don't have the strength any more."

"No, that's not true. It's no use."

"It doesn't matter to Nathan any more either."

"OK, good for you – go if you still believe."

"If you still believe it's of some use, I mean."

"I believe in it, yes; I believe in it, but only up to a certain point."

"In any case, our demonstrating serves no purpose."

"Perhaps you will persuade someone, but what can that 'someone' do?"

"What's really changed in all these years? What progress has been made?"

"Vered, you know yourself that it's only got worse. On both sides. And I'm tired."

"No, it's not that… I'd tell you if it were that."

"OK, I'm depressed. Of course I'm depressed. Aren't you? Who isn't?"

"No, look – the truth is, we've become a people of depressives. At one time I would have got angry with my daughter because she doesn't even follow the news. Myriam never takes an interest in anything, you know that, don't you? But now they all seem to be the same."

"Yes, in my office too."

"You see?"

"So you're saying I'm right…"

"You see?"

"That's what I'm telling you: we are a people of depressives."

"Yes, OK, I'm speaking for myself. Let's say I'm

speaking just for myself, but it's the truth."

"No, this time I can't do it. I've always followed you, haven't I? I've always said you were right. But to tell the truth, I don't even know... I mean ... perhaps all I wanted was for someone to tell me what to do, that's all. But now I don't feel like making the effort any more."

"I'm really tired. At nights I don't sleep a wink. If I think about Nathan, who still has over two years..."

"I don't know. He's certainly changed."

"Nothing seems to matter to him any more, that's what hurts the most. No, that's not true. That's not true: what's killing me is my fear for his life, every minute of every day and night. I can't stand it any more."

"Yes, we always said that."

"He's changed."

"It's true. A few years ago, out of all of us Nathan was the pacifist. Now it makes me laugh to think of it. Or maybe it makes me cry, what do you think?"

"He went off to serve believing in it; he felt it was his duty. He went with his friends... With his schoolmate... You knew about that, didn't you?"

"Oh, Myriam... Myriam is another worry. Since that other awful business, she's not been herself. She doesn't even go to the gym any more, and you know how often she used to – how important it was to her. Now in the afternoons she just visits that hill, where she used to go with her friend."

"Yes, I am, I'm very worried. But I don't know what to say to her; I don't know what to think any more. I no longer know what to hope for myself, so what do you want me to say to them? What's left for us to say to them?"

"That's true. I've begun to think the same. I'm beginning to see it like that too."

"Maybe we should just stay apart, each defending himself from the sight of the other."

"It depends on how you look at it. They leave us in peace, we leave them in peace."

"Yes, it's true, I'm very depressed. But as I said, we're all depressed."

"That's just how it is. We are depressed; they are desperate."

DIMA FORCES HERSELF TO REMAIN GLOOMY

Having finished the equation, Dima tried to distract herself as she awaited the result, but her thoughts reacted to the spring air coming in through the window. The return of spring immediately took her back to a day last April, when she and Faris had gone out alone and walked as far as the walls of Beit Jala.

The wall in front of the school was rubble. She had to think of rubble.

Rubble.

As much of it as she wanted.

In the middle of one night a bulldozer had driven through the streets of the camp. You can hear a bulldozer from quite a distance, and it takes ages to move through the streets of Dheisheh. The slow, sinister sound was as familiar to her as the rest of the soundtrack of the occupation. As familiar as the Apache helicopters, as the tanks, as the smashed-in doors, as the gunshots.

That time the bulldozer had stopped in front of a house not far from hers. The family who lived in it had just enough time to grab the children and get dressed before the soldiers blew up their home. They had used perhaps twice as much dynamite as was necessary and the ferocious blast had carried as far as Dima's house, sending rubble falling onto its roof.

Incredibly the bathroom of the demolished house had remained intact, but the bathroom door had ended up lodged in the wall of the house opposite. And around the dispaced door someone had written: *Even if they bombard this house they will still be unable to take what I love most.* All their photos had blown away from the ruins of the house, and kind neighbours had later picked them up. Their wedding photo, for example, with the photographer's name printed on the back, and the place: Jerusalem, Jordan.

Now the family lived in a tent with the Palestinian flag fluttering above it; plastic chairs, carpets and the coffee pot. Sa'ana, one of the women, frequently suffered panic attacks.

At her desk Dima tried to look like she was paying attention but her mind raced with a mad whirl of images.

Until she was eleven she had lived closed up in the camp. With another eleven thousand people. In less than half a square mile. A barbed wire fence surrounded them, and there were ten gates but only one was open. Coming in and going out was long and difficult because of the checks, so she did it late and seldom; and it was only when she was older that she understood what someone had sprayed in paint on the outside: *It's cheaper to kill them.*

After the fence had been removed, Dheisheh became open, but not even the pleasure of new discoveries could erase that warm and bitter sense of separateness. Dheisheh was her home, a world apart. A world in waiting. Far from Bethlehem, where she would go to live after the wedding and which was in fact practically next door, even closer than Jerusalem, eight kilometres further up. In purely geographical terms her grandparents' villages were even closer, although no one had ever seen them because they were unable to return. But her father always talked of those villages on the days when the Jews celebrated what they call the War of Independence and the Palestinians call the *Nakba* – the catastrophe – when they were driven from their homes. It was on one such occasion, sitting down at their table, that her father handed his eldest son the key to his father's house in the village, just as his father had once given it to him. But first they would have to see if the house still existed.

"Upon retirement, how many Jews will I have killed if I kill one a day every working day for forty years?" the old maths teacher was saying, repeating a familiar joke, and the class laughed and – satisfied – made their calculations. Dima lowered her head, crushed by a weight she could no longer bear.

With an enormous effort, she once more turned her thoughts to Khaldun and Ibrahim.

GHASSAN CHECKS THE CONTENTS OF THE BAG

Six metal bottles, the kind they used in hospital. A bit dirty and a bit dented. Rizak had told him he had found them in a dump. In each bottle he had put some explosive and a mercury lamp with a twelve-volt battery. Then he had taped them to two small mortar bombs, which he had bought from a shepherd in ash-Shawawra. Finally he had connected everything to a firing button.

Boy, Rizak certainly knew how to do a good job. Ghassan had to admit that he had never learned to prepare bombs like this. Rizak was better at it – especially at picking things up here and there and adapting them to the purpose. It had been a good idea to ask him to lend a hand this time. Not that Ghassan didn't understand explosives; he did. You could even say that he liked them

– a lot. He liked to imagine the strength of the blast that lurked inside. He liked their smell and their texture; he could always feel them under his skin.

The first time they had given him explosives, Ghassan was fourteen and had only been in Dheisheh a few months. He had come there with his family after the Oslo Accords, from the refugee camp in Lebanon where he was born and raised, just like Rizak. Today, nine years later, he still hadn't got used to the fact that he was finally in Palestine, but at the same time he wasn't there yet. You could say that he had been happier in Lebanon: at least there it was easier to dream.

So it wasn't long before they gave him explosives, and by sixteen he had already had an accident: a grenade had exploded too close, and a few fragments had pierced his forehead and left eye. Since then he had suffered from terrible migraines, which mostly occurred on days like this, when the weather changed. But Ghassan never felt anger towards that grenade, nor towards the person who had given it to him. On the contrary, he felt that those fragments which remained in his head had charged him with power, giving him a surplus of trapped strength, ready to explode to order.

Already this year Ghassan alone had planted a good six explosive charges in various parts of Jerusalem, and things had only gone wrong that time at Ghilo, when the guards of the Mishtara had fired at him and he'd had to flee with a bullet in the leg without managing to trigger the explosion. Otherwise he was the precise type – he knew how to time things and didn't allow his nerves to get the better of him. Nothing compared with the moment when he set off the device: his rage exploded into the sky and for a moment he felt as if he had won a truce.

He opened a cupboard and pulled out a woman's shoulder bag, the kind with two long handles. Carefully he placed Rizak's explosive device inside the bag and threaded the firing button through a pocket in the strap. It seemed to him that the thing should work. It was easy to reach the pocket, and the bag didn't seem either too full or too heavy. He put it back in the cupboard and kicked Rizak's empty bag under the bed.

Then he went to watch the video recorded the day before.

SHOSHI RECEIVES ANOTHER PHONE CALL

After her conversation with Vered, Shoshi felt even more exhausted. It seemed as if fate had decreed that this morning she should remain sitting on that chair. She couldn't move.

They had returned to Israel with ideals. Where had they ended up? Why was it that a Jewish mother no longer knew what to say to her children?

The phone rang again.

"Nathan! How are you? In Jerusalem? Why Jerusalem? Wait, I'll come and pick you up... Right now. Wait for me in that bar on the right, just as you come out of the station... Actually, it might take me a while; I'm not dressed yet. But wait; I'm coming."

Nathan on compassionate leave. Nathan in Jerusalem. She didn't even pause to wonder why. All her strength came back to her. She slipped quickly under the shower, towelled her hair without drying it, dressed, picked up the car keys and headed for the bus station.

10 A.M.

Myriam is on the Hill

Up on the hill it was still wet but the sun gave the earth a particular scent. From there Jerusalem seemed to lie quietly, waiting to be noticed from above. Myriam looked down over the Knesset, the Gan Sacher, the Rehavia district.

Since the day they had buried Michael's arm, she could no longer bear to feel closed in, anywhere. Their flat, for example, on the outskirts of Jerusalem, so packed with African furnishings and thousands of photos of America, and so small that if you took two steps you were already back at the door. The school entrance hall, always so full that you had to jostle your way through. The gym with no windows and the air that kept all the sweat inside. Clothes so tight that it took an effort to put them on and pull them off.

Yet she had earned those tight-fitting clothes. She

had paid for them with months of workouts in front of a Jane Fonda video, and an uncompromising diet that had slimmed down her waist, hips and bottom, and won her the looks of Joseph, Moshe and even Aharon, who was gorgeous and right out of her league. An apple in the morning, salad for lunch, chicken in the evening. Checking herself out in the mirror thirty times a day. Weighing herself on an empty stomach. Measuring herself. Trying on outfit after outfit before deciding what to wear. Getting up half an hour early each morning to give herself the full make-up treatment: foundation, blusher, powder, lipstick, mascara and eyeliner. Watching her face change, take on the shadow of a woman and glow as if she were happy.

That had been her life, and only two months had passed since that life. Two months since Michael's flight.

Like Myriam, Michael had wanted to go away. They both wanted to go away. "We are Americans," they would say to one another. "What is there here for us? Sooner or later we'll leave." Michael really was American; he was born in Texas and so was his mother, whom his father had met in Paris. But one day his parents got sick and tired of McDonald's, the long cars and the long roads, the gangs in their suburbs. They remembered the Promised Land.

For her part Myriam felt American because they had moved to California when she was only four months old, because of her father's job, and hadn't returned to Israel until she was twelve. And whereas her older brother, Nathan, who was almost fourteen at the time, had been able to study Hebrew for a year before starting his new school, she, being younger, had gone straight into hers. It hadn't been fun, feeling excluded from everyone's games for almost a year. And, since then, it had been so much effort, always, to keep up with the others in her schoolwork.

"It's so miserable here," she complained constantly to her mother. "When we gonna go back to California?"

Since her husband had left, moving to Tel Aviv and leaving her alone in Jerusalem with the children, since everything around her had become so difficult to understand, even Myriam's mother had begun to ask herself, When we gonna go back to America?

It wasn't just the language – other things in this country made life unpleasant. The armed soldiers who filled the streets, for a start. It had been one of the first things Myriam recalled seeing, newly arrived from America; still only young, it had frightened her. It was the years following the first intifada. Her mother had tried to explain it to her – as much as an adult feels like explaining to a child. And she had made that little do for always; she simply never wanted to tackle these issues.

* * *

"What does it mean to say we're Jews?" Myriam and Michael would ask one another many times, in heated disagreement with others and their certainties. "Why do we have to stop being American to go back to being fundamentally a Jew? Why at a certain point in life do we have to?"

And everything was miserable in this city of "fundamentally" Jews, especially compared with California's open faces and broad shoulders; the noisy laughter; the bellies and backsides wobbling under clothing; the toys in the shop windows; the big bars; the neon signs and strong colours. Here everything was white and monotonous, and black, and dry, and miserable.

Physically, though, Myriam was not exactly built like a Californian. Her paternal grandparents had come from Morocco, and like them she was petite and dark. Very dark. Grandfather had arrived in the Promised Land in 1946, when he was eighteen. Together with a group of his countrymen, he had rolled up his sleeves and begun to till, plough and harvest. Her maternal grandparents had been here even before then, since 1943, having fled the pogroms of Eastern Europe. They too had learned to work the land. And to get hold of rifles and machine pistols, and hide them under the sheaves.

* * *

Abu Said was born in August 1948 in the middle of the road. His aunt had used a stone to cut the umbilical cord that bound him to his mother, and his father had buried the placenta at the side of the road and then smiled at everyone, because at that moment he was happy. A few hours earlier, they had switched off the gas under the pots already fragrant with roast and fled from their village, terrified by the arrival of squads of armed Jews prepared to stop at nothing. It took days for them to realize that they wouldn't be able to return very soon, not even to get their linen and dishes. Aatra was the Arabic name of their village, but you won't find it on any map today.

The building site in Jerusalem opened at seven, but to get there on time Said had to leave the Dheisheh refugee camp before four. The army checkpoints were unpredictable, and at the Bethlehem one, in the dark before dawn, there was always a winding queue of vehicles and men. For a lifetime Said had been crossing military checkpoints. And for a lifetime he had been spending his days with Jews. He had been a foreman with the Israel Barzilai construction company for five years.

"This intifada won't end soon," Jacob was saying that morning as they put up the scaffolding. "There are people just waiting for a chance to start again. It won't end soon."

"Anyway, we knew they were ready," Gabriel said

bitterly, tightening the clamps with all his strength. "All these tales of provocation…" And he shook his head and stopped to make a gesture with his hand, as if to say: what provocation?

Jacob added, "Right – and where do all these weapons and explosives come from? They can hardly collect them all in a couple of days. Response to provocation, my foot!" And he too tilted his head to one side and raised his chin, and as he did so he glanced at the sky to take a look at the weather.

Said remained silent. They were used to holding this kind of conversation in front of him, and they didn't go over the score. Above all they never uttered the words "Arab" or "Palestinian". If anything they said "they", to indicate someone who at that moment had nothing to do with either party.

Gabriel continued. "Fact is they don't want peace, we've seen that."

And Jacob: "We've granted them everything; what more can they want? They don't accept it. Peace obviously doesn't suit too many of them."

"My son complains, says I won't let him have a life," said Gabriel after a while. "He's right too; he's fifteen and we keep him shut up in the house. My father drives him to school, every day, there and back. At fifteen! One time when he had to go on the bus I can't tell you how I felt – nervous as a cat with fear I was that day. Cinemas and

56

discos are out of the question, and now I don't even let him wander through the shopping centre. He complains, says I won't let him have a life."

Jacob nodded in a token of understanding. And all the while they carried the planks to the scaffolding, according to Said's instructions.

Old Said was dignified and patient. He was fifty-four but looked sixty-five. A lifetime of crossing military checkpoints. A lifetime of days spent with Jews.

GHASSAN IS SATISFIED

Ghassan finished checking the video and then wrapped it up, writing on an address in capitals. If all went well, by the afternoon little Samir would take it directly to the offices of al-Arabiya. Once more his chest swelled with pleasure. He had arranged everything, and he was almost ready. He fingered the two medallions he always wore around his neck: one held a photograph of Saddam, the other the pope, taken when he had come to Palestine and met with Arafat. At certain moments these medallions gave him encouragement and solace.

Today he was not acting as Private Ghassan. In addition to Rizak, Adum and Mustafa were also lending a hand, together with their younger brothers, who had their own small tasks to carry out. Today Ghassan was a general. Capable of making a far more powerful explosion. Of creating panic and an unparalleled blurring in the world.

Boom! And skies would fall on heads, hell's gates would open, and all would be clean again for a while.

Boom!

Peace. Peace for Ghassan.

11 A.M.

ABRAHAM THINKS AGAIN ABOUT THE LOOK OF THE ARABS

The supermarket was packed. For Abraham the buzz of the customers and staff inside blended with that of the children and their grandparents – and the crows – in the park across the way. Also, at around nine, two Arab women had set up a stall there and were selling dates, olives and a great quantity of spices.

Thinking about the scent of all those spices, which he could only imagine because of the distance and the confusion, took him back to his childhood, and he began to think about the land where he was born, and where his forefathers had been born and lived for generations as far back as could be remembered. He had been five when they had left Syria. Too small to understand why. Big enough to preserve its songs.

"We couldn't stay there any longer when the war broke out," his father had explained to him many times.

His father always remembered how they'd had to make a hasty escape, leaving all that they had built up, changing their way of life for ever. "And in any case, when did they ever want us? Even though we were born and died there, we never belonged to that land."

"Why?" Abraham would ask him every time; but he was a little boy, and the answer was hard both to give and to understand.

When his family moved to the new state of Israel, Jerusalem had still been in shock after a war that had severed long-standing friendships. Few Jews and Arabs maintained relations with one another. For example, the Arab grocer in the house on the corner, two blocks away from them. As a small boy, Abraham had spent hours there, practising his version of Arabic, which was somewhere between the childish and the new. Sometimes he wondered how his parents could have closed the door for ever on that kind of warmth, which he still felt belonged to him.

"You're wrong," his father, who was old by then, would say. "You're confused, because you never really lived that life. All you can remember is the voice and the arms of your wet nurse, the good Amin, who gave you her milk for two years, may God rest her soul. But you don't remember the looks of the other Arabs."

Abraham had carried it with him for a lifetime, that Arab look. A flash of recognition and rejection, a clot made of the bonds of collective suffering. A profound, shifty, veiled look. Which was a part of him and a part of them.

Old Sara always joked about this sensitivity of his. "With you we can be sure you'll recognize an Arab from a distance," she would sometimes say to him when they moved him to a new assignment.

This was not so easy for everyone. For an Arab and a Jew can have the same features, the same complexion, the same way of dressing and moving.

But not the look; the look is different.

DIMA REMEMBERS MANY THNGS, THEN ASKS PERMISSION TO LEAVE

On the thirtieth day of the curfew Ibrahim discovered his father's blood by patting it with his hand several times, and then he rested that hand on his brother's head in order to stand up.

A moment earlier, Marwad had been playing with the two children and Dima had been watching them. She had looked at them without seeing them, in the torpor of that enforced quiet. For a while she had imagined Faris in Marwad's place, and instead of Ibrahim and Khaldun she had seen other little boys.

Marwad had been lucky. Safiya had given him two boys straight away, and they were sturdy. Dima would give Faris little boys, and Faris would be a loving father to them, like Marwad. Then she would give him girls, who would help her look after the house and their father and brothers. In this way her thoughts wandered as the muezzin chanted his song on that sweetly musty evening.

Suddenly there came agitated yells followed by shots, cries and women calling; then shots from closer by, and a screech of tyres right under the window. Soldiers. The soldiers in their trucks had moved swiftly into the camp, on that thirtieth day of the curfew. Dima's head sank violently into her shoulders, as if an unbearably heavy weight had been hurled onto it from high above, while her sisters and sisters-in-law threw themselves into a corner like rags and the men stood up in alarm behind their old father. When the sound of the truck's engine faded, and with it the shots, Dima looked up and could no longer see Marwad.

Instead she saw Safiya, her arms spanning the doorway, pushing hard against the door jamb, her mouth gaping in horror. And after, only after, came the howl; and for a moment, there was a stunned silence, while the howl exploded through the broken window; and then the whole camp exploded in its own howl, a howl from the guts, through clenched jaws, from eyes already swollen.

And as the howl rang out Dima saw Khaldun sitting motionless on the couch looking at the floor. She saw Ibrahim slip down. She saw Safiya hurl herself forwards

64

and huddle down on the floor. She saw herself running down the stairs, her little first aid case in her hand. She saw her cousin Ali, together with a crowd from the street, running up the stairs alongside her and glancing at her case. She saw the room that had been her companion for thirty days and she saw Safiya bent double in a corner.

Then she saw she had put her foot in the blood.

Ibrahim was rubbing his little hands very gently in the puddle of blood. The tiny room filled up as a throng of people flattened themselves against the walls. Her cousin grabbed Marwad, who was lying prostrate on the floor. Dima came up with her case, bent over and opened it. Ali turned Marwad over, and his eyes met Dima's and slipped inside them. Then they were still.

Khaldun climbed down from the couch and he too began to put his hands in his father's warm blood, then he looked around him. His little friend Khaled, who had come running with his mother, started to cry. Before she had time to register it, Dima found herself vomiting violently near the body of Marwad, who was still staring at her. Some of the vomit splashed onto Marwad, increasing the horror and the guilt. Finally Safiya began to wail, and then the yelling started up again, as if from a kind of shock that spread from one to another, venting and magnifying itself.

* * *

With trembling hands and without knowing what she was doing, Dima dug around in her case – she had just finished a first aid course in case of emergencies – as Marwad's eyes continued to stare at her. But her cousin, who still clung to Marwad, looked at her with compassion, then lowered his head over the motionless body and concealed both their faces and his weeping.

What is a news item, Leila? Little Fatwa, who is growing up and puts on her veil for the first time, and who looks so radiant? My father, who has never had land or a village, but who talks about them as if they were the things he has known best in all the world? Lame Abdel always off his head? Marwad, who dies in the house where he has been closed up with his family, and whose children play in his blood and then find themselves in the midst of the terrifying howl of the camp and weep for fear, and whose fate is marked for ever by other people's mistakes?

What can a news item do, Leila? Tear a rent in your guts, suddenly clear your mind, slip a commitment into your heart? Turn your life upside down: the future is what you have today, the past is what you shall live tomorrow.

What is a news item before it becomes news, Leila, when it is still a blend of anger, vengeance, action, suffering, hypocrisy, cowardice, fear, hope, signs? When you come and cook it into news and carry it around the world, it has already lost its strength; you have already stripped it of the howl and the urgency that involves understanding.

Where were you, Leila, that winter's night when the soldiers came to our house and made us all come out – even Eyad, who was only six days old, clutched in Fatima's arms – and we stood there in the cold rain until dawn, pretending still to be sleepy? Where were you when they took Abdel, who used to laugh, and we heard nothing more of him for six months? Where were you every time my father was humiliated by the orders of a soldier younger than his own youngest son?

A lot of things escape you, Leila.

And there comes a point when nothing remains. Not even us two. You left the scene, and when you returned there was no longer a place for you in my life.

I'll give you some news, Leila. For them it is finished. Believing that they're stronger is finished; believing they can do anything is finished. Rooting about in our homes and under our mattresses is finished; rooting about in our lives is finished. The news is me, Leila. All of us will be the news. They'll find themselves in a nightmare; they'll find themselves in a hell. They will *have* to change, because *we* are about to change them.

* * *

The muezzin's call rose up. The moment had come to leave. Dima closed her notebooks and put them in her desk, neatly piled up one on top of the other. She left her pen next to the notebooks, lying exactly perpendicular to them. Then she asked permission from the teacher and went out.

MYRIAM PLAYS A GAME

From above, Myriam looked down on the people tiny as ants who moved around the streets of the city bumping into one another. She began to play a game she and Nathan had invented when they were small: imagining the lives of the strangers passing by.

He's a grandfather who can't find his grandson, Nathan would say, struck by a man walking about anxiously. No, he's an absent-minded teacher who has lost his homework. He wouldn't look that worried about something so small, Nathan would note. Perhaps he's afraid that this time they'll sack him, she would hazard.

And they would continue in this way until one convinced the other, and then they would carry on, telling each other what the grandson was like and where he might have ended up, and what his grandfather would say when he found him again, and what the child's parents would say once they returned home safe and sound.

For a while her gaze followed a particular dot moving

among the others. She's a girl, like me, and like me she hasn't gone to school, Myriam thought to herself. Because she's carrying a secret – one so heavy it makes her stagger. Perhaps we could go fifty-fifty, she said in her heart, on such a heavy secret. And Myriam confided to her, I didn't go to school either, but not because I have a burden inside. On the contrary, right now I have absolutely nothing inside; I'm completely empty. Look, empty! she repeated, defiantly scrutinizing herself.

"You're a mystery to me – I just don't understand you," her mother had said to her two days before as she tried in vain to persuade Myriam to go back to the gym.

Apart from the fact that a mother ought to make the occasional effort – if not, what's she there for? – she was hardly obliged to explain everything to her. Her mother had never understood her; and these days she had thoughts only for Nathan – it had become her fixation, the only thing they talked about at home, since he'd gone off to do his military service. And anyway, what was there to understand? She didn't feel anything inside any more, as if she had been thoroughly hollowed out with a spoon.

No, she didn't feel anything.

She didn't feel anything for Rami any more either – and so much the better. He hadn't been in touch since he left to do his military service. Not that they'd made any promises, but then why had he kissed her like that the evening before his departure? Afterwards she had expected a letter, a phone call; but nothing – not even a text message just to keep in touch. It was strange for Rami to behave like that. But maybe she was even stranger, she who couldn't even say now if she had liked those kisses or not.

When it happened she would have liked to tell Michael about it right away, but Michael wasn't there any more. Michael was always in love with someone – or so he said – but at any rate, he gave the impression of knowing more about these things than she did. Michael was a big expert on emotions; it would have been nice to ask him now what he thought of this business with Rami. He would certainly have had a theory about it, and Myriam might even have accepted it – if Michael were still around.

All the other boys she knew were so depressing, all much of a muchness; there was no one she liked. Having made all that effort so they would take more interest in her, now all she felt was boredom; nothing. A void. What did they have, to make the other girls fancy them so much? You had to work really hard to get an emotion out of any of them. Then there were her girl friends. Such a trial – she didn't even entertain the thought of meeting up with them after school. To do what? All they did was meet in one another's houses just to chat. Great.

It was the same with her family: she couldn't get interested in anything or anyone any more. She certainly didn't feel like worrying about Nathan too. After all, he was only doing what they all did – he would go away and come home like everyone else. And her little brother: what a pain. As he had got older he had become so boring, just like all the others. At first he had been so sweet, but since her father left home he'd grown closer to Nathan, and now he too did nothing but think about Nathan, talk about Nathan, worry about Nathan.

Her mother affected her the least. Myriam didn't feel anything for her. Last night she had even asked her to keep her company in the big bed, but didn't she understand how embarrassing it was to see her like that? What was all this worry about Nathan? When Michael died her mother had shown up at the funeral, shaking everyone's hand, but what did she have to do with it? She had always made a huge fuss whenever Myriam went out with Michael; she'd never understood why they hung out together so much. Goodness knows what she'd thought – maybe that one day they'd catch a plane to America together.

In fact, her mother *had* promised her a ticket to America, a long time ago, once she got her diploma: so this summer. She'd promised to send her on holiday to some relatives who lived there; they'd show her around and she could "take stock", as her mother liked to say. "And if you really like it we'll move there, I promise." As soon as Nathan finished his military service, she had added. *Of course.*

As if to remind her that after the trip Myriam would still have to take her sabbatical year and then would have time to do her own military service.

She couldn't feel anything any more. She felt nothing, except when she was on the hill.

SHOSHI AND NATHAN TALK IN THE BAR

Shoshi and Nathan had taken advantage of finding themselves in the centre of town to have a wander and buy Nathan some new underwear. Then they had decided to go back to the bar where the car was parked, and have a sit-down and something to eat.

"So then, why the surprise?" asked Shoshi. She tried to sound cheerful but she could sense something was wrong.

"I just wanted to come home," said Nathan simply, with a shrug. "But what about you? How come you're not at work?"

"This morning I got up tired, dead tired," replied Shoshi. But the time had come to talk things over, so she added, "And I felt even more tired when Vered called me about the demonstration on Sunday. I said no."

"What demonstration on Sunday?"

"The usual one with Peace Now and the others that Vered is involved with."

"You used to do these things," Nathan reminded her,

72

and she heard a great weariness in his voice.

"That's true, I did. But I don't feel like it any more. I don't even want to think about it. All I want to do is take my mind off it; I'm so tired. And you – this is a wonderful surprise. How are you?"

"Well."

"It doesn't seem like it. I mean, sometimes it doesn't seem like it to me."

"What do you expect me to say…"

"Whatever you want," said Shoshi, smiling. She raised her shoulders, embraced them with her hands and leaned towards him. "You've never said anything about your life there," she added, and without meaning to her voice sounded plaintive.

Nathan was staring into space. But he spoke. Slowly, but he spoke.

"If you want I can tell you about that first day. It wasn't a great start. The first thing I saw when I arrived was a pile of bags on one side and a pile of personal effects on the other. And a man waiting to be strip-searched."

"That's more than justified by what's happening," said Shoshi feebly to fill the silence that followed.

"Yes, you have to check everyone who crosses over," Nathan said flatly. "People are made to partly strip off, and their shoes and bags are passed through the metal detector. Often they have blades hidden in their soles. Everything they're not authorized to carry is thrown away."

"It's not just a matter of blades, is it?" said Shoshi softly, without looking at him.

"No, but that's not what I want to tell you … I mean, about the first day."

Nathan said nothing for a while, and nor did Shoshi.

Then, more resolutely, he added, "The first thing that came to my mind was a scene from the Holocaust."

Shoshi's shoulders sagged and she looked at him with pity.

"I felt like I had got everything wrong. I wanted to come home. I didn't want anything to do with it. I thought of Vered's arguments; I thought of Jonathan, who refused to fly – which was his whole life – so as not to drop any more bombs. And then that awful … *thing* happened."

Nathan fell silent for a long moment. He looked around carefully, his eyes roving about nervously as if searching for something he had lost. Shoshi almost held her breath. Then he continued, in a low, deep voice she had never heard him use before, as if it welled up from inside him – deep inside.

"We've never talked about this thing among ourselves, ever. But everyone … everyone saw Ariel's head fly inside the blockhouse. I don't know who picked it up; someone did. At such a moment, you don't understand anything any more. You don't understand anything… And then you won't understand it; it's over. That's all you understand – that it's over. By then it's pointless to make any more effort. How can you forget?" Suffering rattled in Nathan's voice.

Silence followed. They didn't look each other in the eye. Shoshi's nose was smarting as she tried not to weep.

Nathan resumed in a firmer voice. "What could they know about Ariel? What could they know about the girl he'd become engaged to two days before we left? What could they know about Abigail, of her violin? They do this to us. Someone thinks it up and sends them to do this to us. The truth is, as far as they're concerned we shouldn't exist!" Nathan raised his voice, and his words rang out clearly.

"Nathan," said Shoshi wearily, quietly. "I don't know if I exist or not any more. Do you believe me?"

ADUM BUYS A BUNCH OF FLOWERS FOR HIS WIFE

Adum was doing his normal rounds while at the same time looking for a suitable place to point out to Ghassan, as they had agreed.

Those white and yellow daisies were pretty, and they didn't even cost that much. Adum thought he'd buy some for his wife. He drew up at the flower stand and got out of the car, and the old Jewish florist gave him a nice bunch for twenty shekels. Adum was already imagining the expression on his wife's face – she would arrange them in a glass and place them on show in the window, and all the women in the house would envy her that day – when he saw the supermarket.

He looked for a quiet place to park, then went on foot towards the entrance. A lot of people were going in and coming out. It must be nice and full in there. The guard outside seemed relaxed.

Adum went back to his car and called Ghassan on his mobile. "I've found a good place," he said.

And Ghassan: "Go back along the entire route and check everything."

Adum started up the engine and drove all the way back to Bethlehem. Then he called Ghassan a second time. "No problems," he said.

They arranged to meet at one o'clock at the marble cutter's yard, on the other side of the checkpoint.

GHASSAN IS IN SEARCH OF PEACE

Peace. That was what Ghassan felt after every explosion. Peace at last. The blast, the trembling air, the pieces shooting away in all directions, the streak of smoke that leaped swiftly up into the sky, and then the fine dust falling back to earth ever so slowly for an enchanted moment. Ghassan didn't hear the cries immediately after; he didn't hear the sirens; he didn't smell the burning; he didn't feel anything at all: only a great peace that slipped down inside him together with the dust from the sky.

*   *   *

What must it be like, living as if you were always stuffed
with explosives? What else could you want if not to get
rid of them every so often? This is how it was for Ghassan, who sought every explosion the way another might
seek an orgasm.

Adum's call had reassured him that all was well. For
his part Ghassan had been ready for a good while. He
had prepared everything; he had forgotten nothing. All
that was left to do now was to give three rings on the
phone: the agreed signal that everything was proceeding
as planned and the appointment was confirmed. Time to
go, therefore – right away.

So?

The video had been wrapped up. The address was written
on it. The bag was in the cupboard. It didn't seem either
full or heavy. The van was waiting behind the house, its
tank filled. What else? Nothing. Had he perhaps forgotten something? The explosive device was perfect; the
weather was dry.

So why didn't he move?

Adum was waiting for him.

The van was behind the house.

The bag was OK.

In the cupboard.

Just give three rings.

He had even remembered to brief Samir. The boy knew where to find the video and what to do with it, and he would keep quiet, otherwise he'd have to answer to his brother. What else? Nothing. All that remained to do was give those three rings and go.

Ghassan swallowed and didn't move.

He thought. Everything had gone very smoothly, fast: very fast. No problems, no unwelcome encounters, no hitches, ever, from the start. A clean operation. Of which he could be proud.

Excellent preparation, Ghassan. But now it is time to move.

Yet Ghassan still didn't move. He had a nagging feeling, as if something were eluding him. Something important. It confused him and he began to feel angry with himself.

He began to pace nervously back and forth, thinking about the bag the van the petrol the video the appointment. He couldn't understand why he was worried. Everything was fine; yet something continued to bother him, buzzing around in his head, paralysing him. Like some vague, feeble worry. Like a niggling complaint, an irritation: think about it *think about it*. But that was strange, because everything was as it should be.

He stroked the medallions of Saddam and the pope that he wore around his neck.

What are you waiting for, Ghassan? What is it that's not right about all this?

He couldn't work it out, so he got moving. He took the bag out of the cupboard and dialled a number on his mobile. He waited until it rang three times, then hung up, slipped his phone into his pocket, picked up the keys to the van, grabbed the bag and left the house.

NOON

DIMA THINKS AGAIN ABOUT WHEN SHE LEFT LEILA

The ground had dried, thanks to a sun that could already kill you at this time of day. Dima took the route that had been decided for her. Ten minutes after she set off, her phone rang three times.

"Don't do it," Leila had urged her when she returned to the screen and understood her intentions. "This wasn't what I meant, believe me. And anyway, I wasn't talking to you. Don't do it.

"It'll take time; it'll take generations... But the wounds *will* heal," she had continued in a low voice.

But Dima had heard her perfectly well. "It'll take time ... but what time, what is time, not something that belongs to us. How long does it take to go from the camp to Bethlehem? Ten, fifteen minutes on foot. Unless you find a tank barring your way. So you stay there for three, four, five hours, waiting, without knowing how long you

83

are waiting for, without knowing why, until you persuade yourself that it would be better to turn back to the camp. So what time are you talking about? Who is it that decides how time passes here?"

Leila shook her head. "I understand you. I understand perfectly. We have to stop; we have to turn back. For too long now we've not been able to see the way ahead. But that isn't enough to warrant your decision. You're just tired, wearied by the long curfew, by Faris's absence – and I must bear much of the blame for that. I shouldn't have left you alone."

"You haven't understood," Dima dared to reply.

"I shouldn't have left you alone during the curfew," despaired Leila, wringing her hands.

"You're right, you weren't here during the curfew – and you should have been, to experience it with us, closed up in here together. Simply talking about it isn't the same thing.

"Imagine being confined to your own home – and it's the same for all your neighbours; the camp is just a big prison with lots of cells – limited to looking out while staying inside. There's trouble if you go out without a permit: look what happened to Rashid during the last curfew. Killed by thirty bullets because he didn't obey the order to stop. He was only taking vegetables home – he had ten children. You can see his photo pinned up on some of the doors in the camp. One, two, even three days go by locked up like this, and then they give you two hours to throw out the rubbish, breathe the air, do the shopping. But if these two hours of freedom, or maybe just one hour, are to be given to you, you will only find out about it just beforehand: the soldiers tell you at the last minute, going around the streets with a megaphone. You can't make plans. Everything in your life is suspended; everything you can or can't do depends solely on them.

"You feel like you're hanging by something you cannot control, and of which you are afraid. You become irritable; you start to feel you are no longer at peace anywhere, not even in your own home. And after a while you notice that you are no longer at peace even when you're alone."

"This wasn't your first curfew and it won't be your last," Leila tried to interrupt her.

"That's where you're wrong, Leila."

"Daylight saving comes and you don't bother to change the clocks – there's no point without school or work. You start living outside time. You forget what day of the week it is. When you rush out to do the shopping, there are interminable queues, and like everyone else you don't know if you'll make it back in time. There's rubbish everywhere on the streets; the dust clings to you and when you come back in you'd like to wash but you can't, because they've cut off the water along with the power.

"Then close to the camp tanks go by and you hear

Safiya, who raises her voice so the children won't hear them, singing 'Rock-a-bye, a new world is coming; dream a little of me.' She sings them things like that. And then you start thinking about what you'll tell your children when they're small so they won't be afraid. But what's even worse is that you start thinking about what you'll tell them when they're big, because they'll grow up: and you won't have anything to say to them. And it won't be long before you become nothing in their eyes.

"My father. Think of my father. My father counts the working days he has lost and says nothing. He tunes in to the news. And he waits, and says nothing. My brothers let their beards grow and compete to see whose will be the longest by the end of the curfew. They wait too, but what are they waiting for?

"Meanwhile the youngest boys play at being martyrs, singing and carrying a mattress on their shoulders as if it were a coffin. 'Honour to the martyrs of Allah! Honour to the martyrs of Allah!' they yell as they leap up and down the stairs with this mattress a thousand times. And in the meantime they've started to wet their beds again. Even the little girls are agitated, they hug one another, they don't talk much, they want you and they reject you. If they play they make a pretend house between two chairs; two of them sit inside it while a third goes *tap-tap*, playing the soldier who knocks and wants to come in.

"We all feel that in some way we are dying."

"It's just a bad patch," Leila said again. "Take some time; think things over."

Dima smiled bitterly. For the first time, she was the one teaching Leila something.

"My father and my brothers…" she continued quickly, gloomily. "My brothers don't speak to him. He brings home the money he earns with the Jews, all of us have always lived on the Jews' money, and my brothers say nothing to him, and in the end it's the Jews who must give us something to live on, something to live on as well as to die on. And you say that this isn't reason enough?"

"It's *not* enough; it's not enough." Leila had begun weeping. "What will you say to Faris? How can you still look him in the eye? What gives you the strength to deceive him like this?"

Dima said nothing for a moment. She thought about it, then said, "Faris should do it too. And he certainly will, he will avenge me."

Leila fell silent with bent head in a corner of the room. By now Dima was talking, Dima wasn't listening any more.

MICHAEL TEARS MYRIAM'S MIND TO PIECES

The hours passed but Myriam didn't move. The clouds scudded busily from east to west. The ground had dried, thanks to a sun that kills the Jews already at this time of day.

Michael had died a Jew, without even being able to ask, "What do you want from me?"

Michael had died a Jew, forcing her now to tackle new questions without anyone to turn to for an answer.

She sat down on the ground, leaned against a tree trunk and took out the booklet of the Tehillim. For a while now she had carried it everywhere with her. Furtively. She didn't go around telling people she carried a book of prayers, but there were some strange ideas in the Tehillim which didn't seem like prayers. They seemed more like insults. Or cries of pain. Or war cries.

So she read: "Lord, you have sold your people for no gain and you have not enriched yourself through their sale." She didn't understand this, yet it *might* be an explanation.

Or: "Lord, you had delivered us unto a place of jackals, and you covered us with the shadow of death."

She also liked to read: "O God, break the lion's teeth in his mouth; shatter his fangs, O Lord."

At least it gave her words with which to express herself; words that she couldn't think up on her own.

There was also a description of cataclysms: "The waters saw you; they were troubled; the depths also trembled. The clouds poured down water; voices came from the heavens; lightning bolts darted. Your thunderous voice was in the maelstrom; the lightning flashed, the world trembled and the earth shook."

What could the waters have seen to be so troubled?

The image of God.

Michael blown up.

Something like that.

Myriam left the Tehillim open in her lap and plunged her hands into the earth as all about her began to spin: the trees, the bushes, the rocks. Everything was moving around her, faster and faster, a dizzying green blur which prevented her from distinguishing outlines and borders; a blur that danced around her, the mad dance of a mad earth, possessed by a sacred frenzy, which had no name, had no masters, as she held on tight with her hands like roots in the earth.

She held on tight with her hands like roots in the earth.

Nothing was worth as much as this earth; nothing was worth as much as this earth, she suddenly thought.

ABRAHAM REFLECTS ON DEAFNESS

The week before, Abraham and Lia had celebrated their tenth wedding anniversary. Abraham was a divorcee; it was his second time around. In fact it was the second time he had celebrated ten years of marriage. But this time it still struck him as the right one. They had invited their relatives and had a barbecue. Lia had made plenty of desserts without milk, as almost all the guests were practising faithful, and it had been a strictly kosher meal. The wine was good, and it had been a fine party. He took pleasure from the memory.

Lia was still beautiful, still carefree. She was twenty-two years younger than he, and when they met he had wooed her persistently. Every morning for almost a year he had rung and asked her to marry him, without getting discouraged. Three hundred and fifty times he had asked her; every morning for almost a year their day had begun like this: a simple question, always the same, nothing else. "Will you marry me?" Until one day, dying with laughter, she had said yes. And since then he had never given her cause to regret it.

Abraham had had no children during his first marriage. Then Lia had given him two boys, although no one had been able to explain why they were both born a little hard of hearing.

"Don't go, Dad," his children had said to him that morning. As they did every other morning.

And, as they did every other morning after he had kissed them, they had turned over in bed without even trying to catch his answer.

So Abraham had whispered to himself, since they

were already asleep again, "See you this evening," and he had closed the door behind him.

He wondered if over the years he had not gradually become a little deaf too. Deaf to all the words around him: he didn't understand them any more. If he ever had. If he had ever wanted to.

What, for example, did those armed soldiers have to say to one another as they waited for the bus across the road? What did that pious one, the Chassid with the peyos, have to say as he argued with one of them? Did they use words that were any use: had they ever been any use, would they ever be? And what did that newspaper have to say this morning, the one the man was reading so avidly on the park bench? From here Abraham couldn't even make out the headlines; but anyway, what use would it have been?

What a lot people had to say, about anything and everything.

But words flew and got soiled, and when they reached their destination they were no longer the same; you couldn't do anything about it. Abraham was a man of few words, and above all he never argued. If he had an opinion, he attached little importance to voicing it; it wasn't with words that he would have explained or, God willing, shared it with anyone. Words weren't enough for something as important as understanding one another. Perhaps it was a habit he had picked up from the children; certainly he had quickly learned to pay heed to other things. To more precise things, clearer than words. To the odours he smelled in the air, for example, like these of the advancing spring. Or of the storm, which he sensed, despite the now clear sky, was still lurking somewhere. To the expressions that revealed people the more they became immersed in their thoughts. To the tiny gestures that some made when they spoke. To glances hidden even to those who gave them.

The expression of that lady who was swiftly crossing the park, for example, staring off into the middle distance. The gesture of that soldier busy arguing with the Chassid; he seemed polite and bored but he would lift his elbow with a little jerk every time the other shook his finger. The look of those Arab women with the spice stall, a deep liquid look, pitch black to be probed, to bathe oneself in.

Maybe it would simply be easier to understand one another if everyone paid attention to looks, expressions and gestures rather than words. Because looks, expressions and gestures have more mercy for men than the words they utter.

DIMA REMEMBERS HER BIRTHDAY

"Listen," said the man with the dark hat and the long peyos, "we need the blood of a Christian child, before Pesach, to make matzo."

"Don't worry about it, Joseph," replied a young man

92

with a disgustingly pale face, "your neighbour Helen's son will do perfectly well."

"But will we get away with it?"

"Don't worry. If anyone becomes suspicious we'll postpone the operation."

A little later the pale-faced young man brought the boy to Joseph.

"Did anyone see you?" asked Joseph.

"No, relax."

"Mummy, Mummy!" cried the terrified child.

"Don't be afraid, my dear," said Joseph. He turned to the young man. "You can go now."

On another occasion Dima would have simply been amused. But that day she had felt a kind of comfort, a relief. She was sitting in front of the television with the youngest children, one on top of the other, watching *The Diaspora*, a long-running series about the history of the Jews broadcast by a Hezbollah station. She was waiting for Faris's visit. It was her eighteenth birthday, barely a week ago.

Although it was hot, the window across the way was closed for mourning. Dima knew that the women were taking Safiya something to eat and weeping with her, but she couldn't hear the boys any more. They seemed dead too.

It was almost as if she were dead with them. In the last two months alone, twenty-one people had been killed in the camp, and death had entered her without asking her permission. When Faris arrived with her present she felt completely dead as she smiled at him, opaque and transparent at the same time. She quietly allowed herself to be feted.

Eighteen is the right age, she thought to herself.

The others were accustomed to counting on her. They expected a lot of her, all of them. Faris most of all. She made them feel proud. That's the way it was in the family; that's the way it was at school. Maybe in the camp too. She had just passed an advanced English course: English was important; she knew it pretty well by now and helped out at the Dheisheh social centre, handling foreign correspondence. Then she had done the first aid course, to help the wounded in emergencies: the more emergencies there were in Dheisheh, the harder it was for ambulances to get permission to enter, or at least to manage to reach a hospital from there. And she was about to get her diploma with full marks: the first, the cleverest, as always. Capable and responsible, in everything. As everyone expected her to be.

This time it was up to her as well; she would do it. It required someone courageous, and not everyone was courageous. It was necessary to find a way to respond to them, to make them pay for death with death. It was up to her to avenge her life and the lives of her father and brothers, who didn't have the strength to do it. And those of poor Marwad and all the inhabitants of the camp. And those of Faris and the children they would never have, because in these conditions there was no future that interested her anyway. She had already been dead for a good while; she no longer had arms, she no longer had hands, she no longer had legs to obey her will. She could no longer continue this life. Nothing interested her any more: nothing except avenging herself. She had to avenge herself; she had to do it. She had to show that any one of them had the strength to do it.

So, while on the screen Joseph offered his unleavened bread to the rabbi and, satisfied, wished him a Happy Pesach, Dima carried on calmly watching her Faris but she no longer saw him.

And at noon on this special day, completely absorbed in these thoughts, Dima had already covered a great deal of the prearranged route. A few more blocks, and she would meet Ghassan.

SAID DOESN'T REPLY TO HIS WORKMATES

Since "education is the only weapon we have in this life", as Said would remark a few days later to the journalists about the plans he'd had for his daughter Dima, he had been a keen and brilliant student until he was eighteen. He had taken his diploma and achieved excellent marks, then he'd had to give up university to work.

He had found a job as a bricklayer, had soon learned to read plans as well as any surveyor, and over time had become site foreman. He had always worked with the Israelis. He built their houses with them, he ate with them, he chatted with them from time to time in their own language, and occasionally he laughed with them. Out of habit, he neglected to express his own opinion.

"Do you think it'll rain again this evening, Said?" asked Gabriel, looking up at the sky as they stretched their legs for a moment before returning to work after their lunch break.

Said looked at Gabriel's honest profile. He was one of the best workers, a hard worker, and if he talked, he talked about his son. Said recalled the first time he had worked with the Israelis, when he was eighteen; before that he had never met any of them except uniformed soldiers. At the time it had made a strange impression on him. Which had still not passed.

"Let's hope not," he replied. "It seems to me that it rained enough last night."

"This morning my son complained that I won't let him have a life," Gabriel said again. But he didn't expect an answer. After a while he added, "But what should a father say to his fifteen-year-old son?"

Said raised his head. He didn't have one son, like Gabriel. He had eleven of them, seven of whom were still at school. And he was perfectly aware that for the older ones the fact that he worked with Jews was a problem, something that heaped shame upon shame.

But what *should* a father say to his sons? wondered Said to himself.

"This is no life; sooner or later it will have to end," Gabriel concluded. And it was as if he were talking to a brother.

This is no life, Said repeated silently to himself; sooner or later it will have to end.

Life with nothing. His workmates had never heard him use that strange expression to define their existence. But a few days later he would use it with all the foreign journalists who came running in excitement to interview him in the hope that he might explain things to them somehow. Nor would his workmates be able to discuss it with him later, even if they wanted to.

DIMA THINKS GHASSAN IS A FOOL

If Ghassan thought he was using her, he was a fool as well as a coward. She was the one using Ghassan.

Ghassan spent his days waiting for someone to do something important. He was a layabout, an idler, someone who had fun with explosives, nothing more. Good only for putting people in touch, slinking through the camp without anyone remembering having seen him.

It had been easy to put the word about.

"I'm ready for an *amalieh*," she had let it be known around the camp. An operation. A move.

And straight away Ghassan had shown up, the expert.

That's how the camp is, she thought. Like a family, for better or for worse. Your life is there, and everyone knows you, and you know everybody – or at least you think you do, by reputation if nothing else. You use one to protect the other, you use one to spy on another. Everyone values you, but only up to a certain point; they value you as long as you behave like all the others who share this life with you. That's the way of the world; that's the way of the family. If you want approval, all you have to do is what they think you should do.

So by the next day Ghassan had hastily handed her a note naming a street and a time. When they met up at the designated hour and place, some people had seen them, but no one too close to her father.

They had exchanged a few words.

"I want to do something," she said. "I am ready for revenge."

That had been barely three days ago. Ten days after the end of the curfew.

Since then she had begun to feel better. She had set to floating through life, suspended and alien, looking at everything with a clean eye. And at the same time, she felt capable, active and alive again. Out of the paralysis of suffering, out of the daily humiliation. Finally in charge.

And now here was Ghassan waiting for her, with his one brown eye and his one blue eye, in a red van at the end of a deserted street, just as he had confirmed with three rings half an hour before.

GHASSAN PICKS DIMA UP IN HIS VAN

"I want to do something. I am ready for revenge," she had said on their first meeting.

He had only given her a brief glance but it had been enough. He had already spotted her the night Marwad died. He hadn't been mistaken; the girl no longer had any blood. She had arrived.

So he trusted her, even though you could never really know with women; sometimes they seemed ready for anything, sometimes just as ready to do nothing. Barely a month before, they had all nearly got into trouble because of a woman who had set off, and then come back.

This time, therefore, he had tried to move as fast as possible. Two days after their meeting he had sent Rizak's little brother to approach Dima outside her school and get her mobile number. Then Ghassan had made her an appointment to record the video, in the back of Mustafa's shop. The girl had come on time, and had shown that nothing surprised her.

All this had happened only yesterday, and, seeing her arrive today with a determined gait, dressed in Western clothes and with her face uncovered, Ghassan told himself that he would run every operation this quickly from now on.

He got out of the van and looked around: no one. He opened the door and Dima climbed in. He closed the door again. There was still no one around. Without saying a word, Ghassan started the engine and made his way down an unpaved side street. Deserted. He stopped once more at the side of the road and said, "This is the bag."

He took it out from under the seat and showed it to her. Dima said nothing. Ghassan opened it.

"Look," he said. "The button is inside this strap. When you find yourself among lots of people, press it."

Dima nodded.

"I can't take you there," he added. "You'll have to walk through some fields. You'll have a good view of the whole road from there. Cut across the hill to avoid the checkpoint. We'll meet up again in front of the marble cutter's – a friend will be waiting for us there."

Dima took the bag, got out of the van and set off.

As Ghassan watched her leave, he felt enormously calm.

"When we arrived in this land, Nathan, we arrived too tired. We arrived after more than two thousand years of persecution, after the Shoah, which killed one in two of us. The Shoah, which, apart from the suffering, the bitterness – an atrocious bitterness – and the terror, left us with a sense of shame. The shame of not having been able to defend ourselves, of having allowed ourselves to be led like lambs to the slaughter. Of not having protected the million children led to the slaughter with us. One million, Nathan!"

As Shoshi spoke she stared at a crumb on the table. Nathan said nothing. Around them people came in one after another to sit down at other tables; they ordered, ate, then went away again. Their day continued, while that of Shoshi and Nathan had suddenly become suspended. Shoshi's voice was heavy. She spoke slowly, lost in the immense effort of tying up loose ends.

"Perhaps it's in our DNA by now – fear, rejection. Destruction. Who do you think came to populate the land of Israel? Idealists ... the traumatized ... dreamers ... fanatics... Men who thought to build themselves up by working the land, something they had never done, to rediscover strengths that had perhaps been lost. And we are their children, Nathan."

Shoshi's voice was both a whisper and a lament. She stared into the distance. Nathan looked at her. And as he saw her gradually immerse herself in this suffering, he felt himself re-emerging from it.

"We swore it would never happen again; you know how we say: no more Masadas. Never again, Nathan. We came here from all over the world; we practically invented a language with which to talk to one another. But we already understood one another, because a destiny like ours is a bond stronger than any nation."

She fell silent once more, but she didn't expect her son to reply. Then she shook herself, and said slowly, but in a high, clear voice, "We have an obligation towards our past and towards the future. We need land, space, to feel safe. You can't feel safe in a strip of land you can drive across in three or four hours, and which is surrounded by people who hate you."

Nathan looked at her again, then he asked, "How long have you felt like this?"

Shoshi shrugged and returned his look. "It's not easy to say, you know. It's not easy."

1 P.M.

DIMA WALKS ACROSS THE FIELDS

Dima took the track through the fields. She was wearing jeans and her long hair hung free; a breath of dusty wind rose up to caress her temples and slowly slipped in among the smooth black hair. She was beautiful, with those big bright eyes that had stopped asking questions yet drunk in all that was offered them, until it hurt too badly and they became like glass.

The ground had breathed out the last of the damp and was once more dry and dusty. As she walked over the barren hill, Dima could see the houses of Jerusalem still and waiting. She lengthened her stride. As she walked, her body became charged, grew harder, like a suit of armour. The soles of her feet grew tougher too, tougher than the rocks that protruded from the red earth. Her brain was hardened and vigilant, like a wild beast ready to spring. Her lungs hardened. Her breath became short, dense, the breath of the desert. Blood mingled with shovelfuls of desert soil.

An emptiness engulfed her; as she moved forward, she felt as if she were advancing into a void. Nothing could reach her. Finally nothing could reach her any longer. Her body was so charged, it could sweep away everything around it. She was charged with an inexpressible power.

Her fist on the strap, she clutched the bag slung over her shoulder.

A red van was waiting on the other side of the Bethlehem checkpoint. From her vantage point she could already see it.

MYRIAM CELEBRATES HER SHABBAT

Nothing was as important as this land, despite its being so confused, with its uncertain boundaries and hard-won identity. Once more Myriam felt the trunk pressed hard against her back, while all the surrounding trees, weary of running amok in her mind, slowly began to return to their places.

When a baby was born in Israel, she recalled, the father would often plant a tree and give it the child's name, and the child would grow up with the photograph of the tree on the wall beside the bed. She realized her hands were still plunged firmly into the earth, and she thrust her fingers in even deeper. Now she was breathing directly through her hands, from the earth. And she felt that this land was their land, just as their fathers had promised. The sky looked down on her.

Yes, this land was beneath them, in this part of the world that was their home. Somewhere in this land the roots of her tree clung deeply to the earth. And each of the trees around her was someone's tree, a tree that had put down roots here and here rose up towards the sun.

Michael too was somewhere, around here: and he had certainly come to the same conclusions. Michael had ended in this land. By now he could no longer leave.

Neither could she.

All was still now. The patch of trees barely trembled around her. It seemed to her that it was already Saturday, when time stops and you feel closer to eternity. Today was her own personal Shabbat, and she would celebrate it all the way.

She thought about when her father had still lived with them.

Her mother had stopped being religious a long time ago; and since her father had left home, little by little they had forgotten all the customs, even eating kosher. But when her father had been there, Shabbat had been untouchable. They would light the candles, recite the prayers and share the wine and the salted bread. No one did anything on that day, and it was nice just to spend time together and talk.

Come to think of it, her father's words had been special.

"God is you," he would tell her. "He is you when you read a poem in your room. He is you when you learn something new. He is you when you say no to arrogance, when you refuse to condone an injustice."

These were the things her father would say to her on those Shabbat days.

It was now that she suddenly felt sweep over her all the grief she had never allowed herself to feel since he had left home. A knife began gradually to dissect her breast, her weeping heart. She surrendered herself to it.

Along the way she had lost many things that could have been hers, but when? Without even noticing, without even understanding. She missed her father. She missed him very much. He would have helped her – now that she understood his words better.

She rubbed away the tears that had fallen under her chin. I am God, she said to herself. If there was an energy that made the grass sprout from the earth, that same energy could also run through her and take her far. Although she didn't understand how, she felt that something was changing.

Around her were only crows, cypresses, olive trees. But the answer was gradually making its way inside her.

Dima had left Bethlehem and the checkpoint behind her; the hardest part was done. Now the path led downhill and entered a patch of bushes, concealing the red van from view. When she emerged from it, she would find the agreed place just behind her.

All of a sudden she felt tired, and she became aware that the bag was heavy and the strap was cutting into her shoulder. She was tempted to stop for a moment and carefully lay the bag on the ground so she could massage her aching shoulder and stiff arms. No one would see her if she stopped. She wanted to stop, she felt extremely tired, she could stop in the shade for a few minutes. Just like that, without thinking about anything.

But her feet carried on taking one step after another. With horror she realized she was no longer in control of her movements.

As the crows cawed at her and the view opened out again towards the marble cutter's, she could no longer stop.

MYRIAM LOOKS UP AT THE SKY, THEN REMEMBERS THE SHOPPING

In a few days the celebrations would begin for Pesach, the Jewish Easter. Once again, at table with all her relatives on the first night, it would be her youngest cousin's turn to say, "Why is this evening different from all the others?"

"Because on this day we were freed from slavery in Egypt," would be the answer, repeated every year without variation. One year her father had added, "This evening we celebrate the fact that we are heading towards freedom, but to what extent are we really free?"

To what extent are we really free?

Myriam looked up at the sky. The last rain clouds had finished their journey westwards, leaving only blue.

What is freedom? Where is freedom? How can we exercise freedom?

Some minutes passed before she decided to check her watch. It was time to go. She thought about making it a long walk and returning home on foot instead of catching the bus. She had the time and the inclination. But along the way she remembered that today was her turn to do the shopping. So she only made it to the first stop, then she caught a bus straight to Kiryat Yovel.

DIMA IS IN THE VAN WITH ADUM

When she arrived at the marble cutter's, Dima saw that there was a white car parked beside the red van. Ghassan and Adum stood waiting for her. As she walked towards them with the weight around her neck, she noted that the two men were looking at her with admiration and respect, as if they envied her, as if she were about to embark on a journey that was forbidden to them.

They had nothing to say to one another, and there were loads of soldiers near by. Dima saw Ghassan take the keys to Adum's car and realized that Adum wouldn't want to risk compromising himself by using it to take her to Jerusalem. Instead she and Adum got into Rizak's red van, and left.

As they rolled along in the van, which was noisy, dirty, with torn upholstery, rickety seats and ancient clutter, Dima felt as if all her strings had been cut. Disconnected. She couldn't even sense the air around her any more. She was sure that if she were to touch any part of her body at that moment, she wouldn't be able to feel it, so dead and frozen was everything. The only thing she could feel was the tips of her fingers and toes; they were hurting, as if the blood had stopped there and refused to do its rounds. She sensed a scent of death all around her.

At one point Adum broke into her thoughts. "Roll down your window," he told her. "Haven't you noticed that awful stench?"

There was indeed an acrid odour in the van, that's what it was. The stink of explosive had spread, the smell of a bomb.

Dima opened her window. "How much longer?" she asked.

"We'll soon be there."

"What's the place? Will you show me where it is?" asked Dima.

"We'll be there in five minutes," he replied.

They said nothing for a while. The five minutes passed, but still they weren't there.

Then Adum asked, "Where's the button?"

"There's a little pocket inside the strap," replied Dima without moving her head, but bending down towards the bag.

"Don't touch it, otherwise we'll be blown up," said Adum.

"OK."

"Keep the bag far from you, keep it far away from your hands and feet, if not we'll be blown up," he repeated.

"OK," she said again.

They had arrived. Pulling up, Adum told her, "If you go straight on from here you'll come to some steps. Go down them and you'll find a supermarket on your left. You'll see it; you can't go wrong."

He added, "Go into the supermarket and press the button."

Dima got out of the van without a word and set off.

The bus was crowded at this time of the day, but Myriam managed to carve herself out a comfortable corner, leaning against the back. She glanced around her and saw only tense faces, so she turned back and looked out of the window. A taxi crawled along behind, driven by an Arab cabbie.

She wouldn't take her sabbatical year, she decided, suddenly clear-headed: who could make her? Deep down her mother would be glad too; money had been scarce at home recently. Above all, she thought, she wouldn't do her military service. It wasn't unavoidable: she would plead conscientious objection, which was possible for girls; it would be enough to say that her religious beliefs forbade her to live and work with men.

Why not? It wasn't unavoidable.

Funny she hadn't thought of this before.

It would mean she could enrol at a graphic design school next year, right after her diploma. She liked the idea of graphics school, she had done for a good while. There were no subjects to be learned by memory, she believed, and the work would be fun. It was just that she had never really thought about it until now; this was the first time she had seen herself so close to it.

She would make new friends, maybe interesting ones.

And she would soon find a job – why not? – maybe with a newspaper. It wouldn't be bad. She would call her father every now and then, and occasionally go to visit him in Tel Aviv. What did she have to do with what had happened between him and her mother?

Sooner or later she would get over her grief for Michael.

She would grasp the sense of what was around her. She would learn to understand what was part of her. And what wasn't.

That's what Myriam was thinking on that bus journey; and suddenly America had disappeared from her future.

DIMA IS OUTSIDE THE SUPERMARKET

There was a guard in front of the supermarket, and when the sliding doors opened, Dima could see another one just inside. A double line of defence. She began to wander around the park opposite the supermarket. By now she no longer felt anything. She didn't hear the birds calling to one another from the trees in the park, or even the heavy beating of her heart. She was simply ready. She concentrated on her task.

A double line of defence. But they didn't necessarily open all the bags. Some people greeted the first guard with a smile as they entered. They must be regular customers, she thought. How to get past? Maybe by walking purposefully past the first guard, putting one foot forward to open the sliding doors. But how to get past the second guard and in among the crowd thronging the aisles and cash desks?

She had to blow herself up in the middle of a crowd. She had to blow up a crowd.

She wouldn't be doing it if she weren't sure she would kill lots of them. She would postpone it. Her life was not worth a few lives; it was worth a great many Jewish lives – at least a hundred. She would blow herself up and take a hundred people with her. A hundred Jewish families would have to suffer what they as Palestinians were suffering. And finally the camp would celebrate. The return of honour. Of a little justice. In the camp they would celebrate the hundred dead together with her martyrdom, which had made it possible.

She was claiming honour and justice, and she had more than a few injustices and humiliations to avenge. At least a thousand, suffered every day by each member of her family. She would avenge every one of them; at a single stroke she would make them remember every one. And she would do it in such a way that the injustices would burn inside them for a lifetime.

At eighteen. Now. She would do it.

* * *

She sat down on a bench. No. If she couldn't do it in the middle of a crowd she wouldn't do it at all. Things should be done properly. Adum had brought her to the wrong place. She wouldn't get past the double line of defence.

Perhaps she lacked courage? No, it wasn't a question of courage. She couldn't care less about dying; she had already decided that it was fine. Today was a good day to die. Too often she had been afraid of dying at the hands of the soldiers, especially when she was a little girl and they invaded the streets of the camp where they were playing and threatened them with their guns. Today she would do it, and it would be her decision to die, not theirs. What she was lacking right now wasn't courage; it was meaning. If she was going to do it, it had to have meaning. She didn't want to do it otherwise; she wouldn't do it.

That was when she saw Myriam. Approaching from the opposite side of the park with a light step and a dreamy expression. Wearing jeans. Small, dark, her hair loose, her eyes gleaming. The first thought that leaped into Dima's head was that she knew her. That girl looked familiar. She reminded her of someone. She couldn't say whom, but someone she knew well. She was sure she had seen her somewhere before... But she was also sure that she was Jewish.

Dima felt irresistibly drawn to her.

* * *

But no one had predicted that those two Arab women would have their stand right there. Why had she only just noticed it? Dima turned towards them. This wasn't in the plan, but it was only right that she should do it.

"Get away from here, now," she said to them, and she said it in such a low voice and with such an imperious look that the two women slipped the loose change they were counting into the folds of their clothing and hastily began to collect up their things.

Then Dima turned once more towards Myriam and purposefully but naturally fell into step with her. The first guard let them both pass, and the sliding doors opened.

2 P.M.

2.05 P.M.: DIMA, MYRIAM, ABRAHAM

What's with those two women? Abraham wondered. From his post just inside the sliding doors he had noticed something unusual. The two Arab women selling spices were hurriedly packing up and leaving – or so it seemed. Too hurriedly.

Abraham's heart froze.

The girl the bag was passing he could only hang on to her to stop her the children the beauty of Lia the sun Amin.

The guard was yelling and trying to stop the girl beside her – Michael's arm; Oh God, Michael! – God, no.

The second guard tried to bar her way. He had blue eyes. Alongside them there was only the girl she had come in with, holding her shopping list.

So they exploded at the same time.

Dima was stretched out with her eyes wide open. She was lying on her chest flat on the floor, her arms spread. "She looked like a Greek statue," someone remarked later.

Myriam had flown across to the opposite side, under a mountain of cardboard boxes.

Abraham was all over the place.

Reported like this it seems as if it happened quickly; and yet it didn't. In that moment, Dima had time to picture the day of her diploma, Faris, the house with Abdelin. Myriam, in reverse, saw California again with all its colours and Jerusalem all white, and she and her father at Disneyland, and finally a curl of convolvulus that was reaching out and all the trees in the photos that carried on growing for her.

Abraham had plenty of time to understand: a Palestinian girl entering with an Israeli girl, same age, same height, same complexion, same features – like sisters. The first guard was local and had recognized the Israeli, who was a regular customer, so without thinking he let them pass together. They both had beautiful black eyes. They both had deep eyes. They both had lost eyes. But in one of them Abraham recognized the look that had been following him around since that morning, for the whole day, or perhaps it had been seeking him for a lifetime. And he even had time to return it.

After the blast and the silence come the cries of horror and the moaning of the wounded. Then the blood flowing and blending with the red paint spilled from the drums at the supermarket entrance. Then the shock of the people who come running. Then the ambulances. Then the panic and the anger and the powerlessness. Then the cursing. Then the strange light that glitters in the eyes of the Arab shoeshine boy on the corner. Then the looks that pass between one Palestinian and another all over the city.

Then the sky of Jerusalem which darkens once more.

THOSE WHO REMAIN

LIA

"That's enough now; it's time to do your homework," says Lia, trying to shoo the children away from the television, which they'd made a dive for after lunch. She goes to switch it off, and at that very moment the cartoon is interrupted by a newsflash.

"A few minutes ago a terrorist attack on the Kiryat Yovel supermarket in Jerusalem. We still don't—"

Lia carries on and switches off the TV. She looks at the children, who have now got up to go and do their homework. She puts a chair next to the phone, sits down and dials Abraham's number. His mobile is silent. She stares at the blank television. It could be turned off, she tells herself. Or the blast might have blown it away. And he can't call me because he's busy helping with the injured.

"I feel he is dead," she says to herself. She remains

motionless and rigid in the chair as the blood begins to drain from her limbs.

How long she stays like that she doesn't know. Then, slowly, she begins to dial old Sara's number.

And already, from the bloodless voice with which Sara answers, she understands.

SHOSHI

Shoshi hears the wailing of sirens in the street below and says to herself, Oh God, Myriam will be at the supermarket now. She looks at the TV but doesn't turn it on. She slips on a jacket but forgets she's still wearing her slippers. She runs to the supermarket. The entrance is in chaos, and already a small group is yelling death to the Arabs, death to the Arabs. There is a security cordon all around the building, but she manages to make her way through and grab one of the stretcher bearers by the arm.

"I'm looking for my daughter," she says to him, and it feels as if she is calm and in control, but her face is frightening, convulsed. The stretcher bearer grabs her to hold her up and to block her view. A few yards away, a man's leg still needs to be picked up.

"No, madam, calm yourself. There are only two fatalities; your daughter isn't here. The terrorist is dead, and unfortunately also a security guard. There are lots injured, but none struck me as serious. I have to get on now."

"Where are they taking the injured?"

"To the Hadassah and Shaare Zedek hospitals for now."

Myriam's mother continues to grip his arm.

"I must go now, madam. You'll find your daughter, you'll see."

Shoshi calls home, speaks to little Dan. Myriam hasn't returned; Myriam hasn't called. Nathan stayed on in town when she left him and isn't answering his mobile. Shoshi calls Myriam's father and asks him to come at once to Jerusalem and call round the hospitals with her.

"I don't know if she's injured. I'm not even sure she was there," she tells him. She remembers the leg on the floor. Panic spreads through her body. Yet she remains rational.

Said

The roar of the explosion carries as far as the building site. As does the wailing of the sirens, and the palpable feeling of pain, and the smell of fear. In the office inside the cabin Said switches on the television. Soon after, the others arrive. The news is still vague. There has been a suicide attack on a supermarket not far from where they are working. There is talk of one death: the security guard. A hero, who, according to the first reports, used his body to block the bomber, preventing her from entering the supermarket, and thus avoiding a massacre. And yes, it was a female terrorist: a woman. In fact a girl.

His workmates watch the television and call home at the same time. Their faces are bleak with a grief that makes them physically sick. Gabriel shakes his head and seems on the verge of tears. The crane operators couldn't come down immediately, but now they arrive. The entire site is at a standstill. There is the silence of mourning broken only by a few disjointed comments. Another one. The supermarket. A woman. They say nothing else.

No one wants to embarrass Said, but no one can manage to look at him.

Oh Allah, how much longer must we atone for the sin of not dying before? Said prays in silence.

The TV camera shows the first few little groups that have assembled near the attack to call for vengeance. Said knows that today in one way or another he will pay. The journey home will be longer than usual, he will have to arm himself with patience. He tries to imagine where the terrorist may have come from and hopes she had nothing to do with Dheisheh. Otherwise a new curfew will prevent him from going to work the next day.

They all seem embarrassed by the fact that he is listening to the news too, so he leaves the room and lights up a cigarette. There are times when they have to stay apart.

* * *

Said is a man who can no longer bring himself to hate. But hatred is nonetheless something he understands. He understands the desperation of the young. He knows that their fathers – he as much as the others – continue to get it wrong. They teach their children important values such as honour above all, the dignity of the person, and – most importantly – respect for the head of the family and the elderly. But before the children's eyes, ever since they were small, their fathers and grandfathers have been submitting to arbitrary checks, curt orders, humiliating searches. Without honour or dignity before the young soldiers. Without an army to join; without ever having been able to fight a real war for their future.

Now their children kill themselves, as long as they can kill their enemy. As long as they can return the terror that they themselves have grown up with. As long as they can square all the accounts with shame. As long as they can show that they are somebody. And their fathers have lost all authority over them. They have grown old before their time. They can no longer do anything to stop them.

What will this girl's act have achieved? Nothing. What idiocy. A girl too: she must have been desperate. With this nothing will change, he thought; on the contrary, it will get worse. Now there will be another school of terror, another wave of repression, and, as a result, other troubled young people, in search of a new vengeance, hungering for martyrdom.

Said glances at his workmates motionless inside the office and realizes that the working day is over. He might as well close the site and each man off to his own home.

SHOSHI

Shoshi and her ex-husband have done the rounds of the hospitals in Jerusalem. They have visited them all. Myriam is not there. They repeatedly ring home. Myriam has not called. Where is she? Maybe she's in shock, wandering around the neighbourhood, and cannot find her way home. They will have to go back to the supermarket, and from there start asking and searching once more.

When they arrive at the supermarket they see that the black Chassidim are already there. The pious ones always turn up last; it's the role they have allotted themselves: with a scraper they collect every scrap of skin stuck to the walls and the shelves, so that it will all have a burial.

And Myriam's parents hear a piece of news that is circulating: there were two terrorists, two girls, perhaps sisters. They have found another one, dead, under a large pile of cardboard boxes.

Two terrorists.

Two sisters.

Two girls.

Two girls.

Shoshi's heart swells unnaturally. It feels hard, almost as if it has stopped. Waiting.

Finally someone comes up to her.

A pain so strong it cannot be described. She doesn't even feel Myriam's father's arm holding her up.

SAID

The camp is in turmoil; the soldiers have come. Many soldiers. Said quickens his step towards home, without hearing orders to stop. When he rounds the last corner, he sees a great many soldiers in front of his house. And the women and children of his family lined up outside.

Immediately he thinks of Amhad, his eldest son. He hopes he hasn't been involved in anything. At that moment, he spots him coming down the stairs handcuffed among the soldiers. He meets his gaze. Amhad. The look his son gives him is so desperate that Said trembles.

FARIS

Faris is on his way from Bethlehem, satisfied with his day. He is walking calmly, along the main road that skirts Dheisheh. He is lucky to still have job offers. Somehow or other things happen for him. Whereas almost all his friends are now unemployed, and even his father is finding it harder every day to get work.

But as soon as he enters the camp, he begins to feel uneasy. An eerie quiet is emanating from all around, a strange sense of emptiness. The streets are deserted, as if a great wind has swept through, but from a distance come cries and uproar. As he nears Dima's house the sounds of the disturbance become clearer – and it's also clear where the inhabitants of the camp have ended up.

First he sees Said, alone, his arms hanging loose, his shoulders bent, his eyes distant; and Faris thinks, He's aged twenty years. Then he sees the house surrounded by soldiers, and the women terribly pale, clutching the smallest children in the middle of the street. And he sees the strange and elusive look of the crowd, a bit further off. Then he sees that none of Dima's big brothers are there.

Amhad, he thinks. Amhad, by Allah, what mess have you got yourself into?

Finally he notices that Dima is not among the women. He takes a better look but he cannot see her. At his gaze the women burst into tears. He still cannot see Dima. He gives old Said a questioning look. Said is gasping. For a moment his lip trembles, as if he too wishes to burst into tears, but he doesn't. He holds his arms out towards Faris as if to welcome him.

Faris thinks, I'm covered in mortar; I can't touch him.

Then, like poison, death slips into his bones and makes his teeth chatter.

THE INHABITANTS OF THE CAMP

When the soldiers leave, having turned everything upside down and taking Amhad and also Melthun away with them – and for Melthun it is the first time – the neighbours begin to empty Said's house, before the bulldozer arrives.

They are all panting as they quickly carry down the stairs the television the coffee table the couch the mattresses the stove, but they are also keyed up with excitement. Only some are immobilized by terror, and they are the ones whose houses are next door to Said's: if the soldiers' bulldozer comes, as it always does, to destroy the martyr's home, then the whole building will collapse, and their homes with it. A rumour begins to spread that there are foreigners, volunteers, who will sleep in Said's empty house tonight, to offer passive resistance to the demolition. Perhaps one of these foreigners will also help them appeal to the Israeli High Court of Justice: they can hardly knock down the neighbours' houses too.

Said is stunned, motionless. They should let him see his daughter's body. They have brought nothing to prove that it is Dima. They have offered him no justification for thinking it is her.

Where *is* Dima, though? They say that she left school before noon with an excuse, and since then no one has seen her. So Dima isn't here; she hasn't come back. Dima hasn't come back.

His wife is now crying out in grief, surrounded by women from the camp who are trying in vain to calm her. The girls are weeping in one another's arms; Amhad's wife is clutching her youngest child to her neck; Melthun's fiancée is looking desperately around her. The younger boys are not crying, because now that the soldiers have taken away Amhad and Melthun, they are the men of the house. All the inhabitants of the camp reassemble, and already they are firing shots into the air to celebrate, and sweets and chocolates appear, and the first rounds of applause and the first toasts begin.

Jihan tells everyone several times that he bumped into Dima that morning. Her schoolmates arrive, and say that over the last few days they found her distracted but affectionate with all of them. They are excited and full of admiration. They are brimming with life. Of all of them, notes Said, who without wanting to is photographing for ever in his mind every moment of this long afternoon, only Rim, Dima's long-standing classmate, is crying. Only she has pity.

Pity, *pity*. Pity for my children, pity for my wife, pity for me, pity for Faris. Why don't you have pity? Why are you celebrating Dima's folly?

* * *

The word goes round that al-Arabiya is broadcasting the martyr's video. They go to watch it at a nearby house. From now onwards the video will be continually aired by other Arab stations at ten-minute intervals.

Yes, it's Dima. It's Dima.

Dima?

FARIS

"May Allah forgive her," says Faris aloud, as all around people come running to congratulate the family. What worse betrayal than death can come from your betrothed, from the future mother of your children, from the consolation of your evenings, what worse betrayal than this?

"May Allah forgive her," says Faris. From her he had expected every happiness. Since they were children he had been in love with her. He was proud of her; he accepted everything about her. Plans, projects, decisions: he knew Dima's worth, and he listened to her.

And she had done this to him.

She hadn't even given him the chance to argue, to defend, to save. She had completely excluded him from her life. She had gone her own way, as if he had been nobody, nothing. Only yesterday they had been talking about wedding plans…

Grief flares up along with resentment and outrage.

May Allah forgive her, says Faris to himself. I certainly won't. She has killed my life along with her own, my future along with hers, all our hopes and dreams.

Meanwhile journalists arrive and ask questions. Someone leads Faris away by the arm to prevent him from talking. The hardliners stay with the journalists, and allow themselves to be filmed as they make toasts.

The TV cameras roll.

Held tightly by the arm by a stranger, Faris tries to run through his last visits to Dima. But at this moment he is unable to reconstruct anything, every now and then he glances at the screen where Dima plays her last part and he doesn't understand.

How could she, his cousin, whom he thought he had known since birth? How could she have organized all this, and with whom, who was the coward who supplied her with explosives, and how could he, Faris, not have seen what was going on? He strives to think clearly, to delve into his memories to work out when it was that he had begun to lose Dima.

Suddenly he thinks that perhaps she was never his.

All around, other people arrive – people he has never met but who knew Dima – and they are celebrating too. They are eating sweets, shouting and making up songs of joy.

And what about this Dheisheh, which his mother has told him about so many times, the camp that "becomes your family, your home and everything in life", as she so often repeats when recalling the years she lived there? Are these the inhabitants who according to his mother are all brothers, even though they come from forty-five different villages? What did their fathers leave behind in those villages, apart from the dream of an orderly life, even their souls? What has this degradation in which they live, generation after generation, brought them that they celebrate the suicide of one of their own? Had they all participated in a mass suicide it would have been better, may Allah forgive me, he adds quickly.

Faris leaves the camp and returns to Bethlehem, taking advantage of the fact that no one is paying him attention any longer. His brother will be home – he probably knows everything by now. Things will be better with him there.

He opens the front door very quietly and hears his brother's voice. He stops to listen.

"Of course. But when you see the people who are supposed to be governing us, the ones we believed in, our heroes, who run around Bethlehem and Ramallah in new clothes and fancy cars, what else can you think about but taking justice into your own hands?" his brother is saying into the phone. "Oh sure, it's all just violence now,

sure; we have even become violent among ourselves…
We have become a violent people, that's true. But when
they've been pointing a gun at your chest since you were
small and you've been subjected to abuse since you were
born, what do you expect to become, if not violent?"

Faris goes over to the stairs and sinks down onto the bottom step. He hides his face in his hands, and since no
one can see him he weeps.

NATHAN

Nathan is sitting on the steps of the Old City. His mobile
lies forgotten in his pocket, turned off. He is too far from
his neighbourhood to hear the wailing of the ambulance
sirens; too absorbed in his own thoughts to notice the
panic that is rapidly spreading through the city.

For hours he has been wandering through the Jewish
and Armenian quarters. Several times he skirted the Arab
district but didn't go in. In the end he sat down on these
steps, and from here he surveys the holy places of the
Temple Mount. In the esplanade between the mosques,
between the Dome of the Rock and al-Aqsa, wanders
a silent crowd of men and women, veiled and wearing
keffiyehs. Below them, Jews rock in prayer in front of
the Wailing Wall: the men on one side, their heads covered with yarmulkes or fur or felt hats; the women on

the other, with kerchiefs over their hair.

The gold of the Dome of the Rock glitters. Maybe Nathan has stared at the sun for too long. Or maybe his gaze is blurred by tiredness and anguish. What's certain is that he witnesses the last rays of the setting sun silently melting the gold of the dome and causing it to pour down the Wailing Wall. Nathan cranes his neck, looking around to see if anyone else has noticed this phenomenon. But the Jews rocking ever more frenetically before the stones of the Wall are too absorbed in prayer to notice anything; and the passers-by are in too much of a rush.

Nathan looks away to erase the image. He gets up and spies the first set of roofs beyond the walls of the Old City. He perceives a musty air, all the fear that stagnates there.

Meanwhile his brother and father are desperately hunting for him to tell him about Myriam.

But this story takes pity on Nathan. It leaves him unaware of what has occurred, surrounded by his own thoughts, carefully sounding out his emotions, still in search of a possible truth as long as he has the time to do so.

LEILA ODER

Leila had an urgent call to the studio early in the afternoon for the transmission of a newsflash. Her shoulder still hurts from the bullet she received a month before, and on days like this, when the weather is changeable, the stitch marks around the scar begin to smart and irritate her again.

She is on air all afternoon, announcing this new suicide attack, and running the video of the young terrorist countless times. In a white veil, her eyes clear and wide, the girl repeats each time: "I will fight in place of the dormant Arab armies who stand by and watch Palestinian girls fight alone."

Leila is tired of this weather and this office in Jerusalem. She is tired of presenting this news item. This evening she gives herself to the TV cameras with a firm gaze and no longer looks her viewers in the eye.

THE WORKERS IN THE MORTUARY

The mother has arrived, says one of the mortuary workers. No, make her wait, not now, is the reply. How can I do that? You can do it. She's right here. Wait, wait. The other two have just finished washing her face and now they're slowly applying face powder, lipstick, blusher. The men work with eyes wide with tears. When they've finished, they pull the sheet tight around the casket.

Shoshi doesn't lift the sheet. She imagines there's little beneath it. Her daughter's eyes are half open, with an expression that strikes her as one of surprise. Perhaps tomorrow, Shoshi has time to think, tomorrow it will be better.

They take her out of the mortuary.

No, we shan't bury her now; not the dark for my shining light. They try to persuade her but she resists with all her might.

Not the dark. Light for Myriam.

LIA

In the meantime Lia is burying her Abraham. In the space of so few hours, you cannot comprehend. When you still feel the warmth of his body upon yours, the body in whose arms you lay only that morning. When you remember the last words he said to you at the door: "I'll bring the meat this evening." When they hand you the dust-covered face of his watch, the strap gone but the rest miraculously intact: stopped at five past two; and you remember the puzzle he left half finished on the table yesterday evening, when he put the little boy for whom he had been trying to assemble it to bed. A puzzle depicting watches and clocks from different eras, showing all the hours of history.

Now Lia can't seem to think about anything else, just this watch that stopped but survived, and the puzzle waiting for her on the table.

When she gets home after the funeral, Lia takes a pair of scissors and very slowly cuts her blouse over her breast – a rent on a level with her heart. Then she lies down on the floor for her seven days of mourning. Someone tries to make her eat, but without success.

GHASSAN

At first it is a migraine, the worst he has ever had. A hideous pain that starts with a pulsating cut at the right temple and spreads across his entire skull through a hundred veins and is so strong that it paralyses his limbs and his tongue, so that even if he wants to shout or bang his head against the wall, he can't.

Then the splinters begin to move. Ghassan is motionless, in a cold sweat, his intestines churning. The splinters have started walking inside his head.

Ghassan's first thought is, They want to get out. But he can't manage to raise his hands to his head to stop them. Terror blends with the pain.

I don't want them to get out, he thinks, panic-stricken. You can't get out, he says to the splinters. You are all my strength, all my anger; you are stuck here, and here with me you must stay.

But they carry on pushing and walking, slowly, forward; and when they can't, a little backwards, or a bit to one side, in search of a way out.

It is a slow, endless, inhuman torture, now joined by nausea, welling up in gushes from his stomach to his throat.

Young Ghassan stays where he is, seated, inert, his arms hanging limp, his handsome yet childish face convulsed, waiting for the inevitable explosion, teeth clenched, eyes goggling.

In the end he manages to shout. It is a frightening shout, which carries across the whole of Dheisheh over the rain that is now beating down heavily, carrying beyond the houses of Bethlehem, leaping over Ghilo to be heard clearly as far as the parapet of Jerusalem, where, lined up in orderly rows on the Mount of Olives, the tombs of the Jews confidently await the day of Resurrection.

"Jerusalem is a dream dreamed together
by myriads of dreamers."

Amir Gilboa

Many news items bombard us each day, leaving us oddly more empty, confused and frustrated – as if the sheer volume of information renders the content meaningless. But sometimes we come across a special piece of news in which we can see a flickering of meaning, and we think that maybe if we delve into it we'll gain some kind of understanding.

I decided to delve deeper into a special piece of news about two girls: one Palestinian, one Israeli. Worlds apart, but – by an irony of fate – taken for sisters. Everyone warned me: if you write this story you'll have to take sides, express a point of view. But a point of view is not a *good* point of view if it only shows one side of the story. Good books don't supply answers. Good books merely help us to ask questions; more and more questions.

What emerged from my exploration of that news item was not just a story about Israel or Palestine, but a universal story. A highly symbolic story, in fact. One that applies to any love-hate relationship; to any tormentor-victim relationship. One that explores that which is more intimate and yet more universal, and which causes us to mirror our enemy. A story that tries our sensibilities and our moral intelligence.

It was a challenge to write; it will be a challenge to read.

Gabriella Ambrosio, 2010

ACKNOWLEDGEMENTS

My thanks to Avigail Levy, mother of Rachel; Samir al-Akhras, father of Ayat; Shoshanna Smadar, wife of Haim; Eid Bassem, Jerusalem; Eyad El Sarraj, Gaza; Gady Castel, kibbutz Sereni; Jonathan Shapiro, Tel Aviv; Michele Giorgio, Jerusalem; Lea Tsemel, Jerusalem; Rachel Lea Jones, Tel Aviv; Rami Elhenem, Jerusalem; Salim Tamiri, Ramallah; Vered Cohen-Barzilay, Tel Aviv; a young blonde woman from the Dheisheh camp; the Israeli students of a school on the border with Jordan and Syria on their sabbatical year before leaving for military service; the Palestinian girls of the youth club run by the Salesian Sisters of Beit Jala; my friends in Italy, especially Luisa Morgantini; and all the others who do not wish to or cannot be named but without whom this story could not have been told.

And, for the English edition, my thanks to Nicky Parker, Amnesty International UK; Bill Shipsey, Art for Amnesty; Donatella Rovera, researcher on Israel and the Occupied Palestinian Territories for Amnesty International; and Sara Wilbourne, Editorial and Publishing Programme, Amnesty International.

And finally a very special thanks to Vered Cohen-Barzilay.

Amnesty International

Amnesty International is a movement of ordinary people from across the world standing up for humanity and human rights. Our purpose is to protect individuals wherever justice, fairness, freedom and truth are denied.

There is a long and terrible history of violence and human rights abuses in Israel and the occupied Palestinian territories (OPT), where Israeli occupation of the West Bank and Gaza Strip has lasted for over forty years. International law is disregarded and it is ordinary Israeli and Palestinian civilians who bear the brunt of the violence. Their suffering is intensified by the ongoing impunity, which means that those who have committed the violations are not brought to justice. People go through enormous stress and anguish on a daily basis. Campaigners in Israel and the OPT, as well as internationally, have tried for years to resolve the crisis. However, without credible commitment to justice and accountability, the chances of a stable and secure future are remote.

The facts tell the story: between September 2000 and the end of July 2007 at least 5,848 people were killed by the conflict. Of these, 4,228 were Palestinian, 1,024 were Israeli and 63 were foreign citizens. Of the total number killed, 971 were children, of whom 88 per cent were Palestinian and 12 per cent were Israeli.

Between 27 December 2008 and 18 January 2009 a conflict between Israel and Palestinian armed groups took place in Gaza and Israel. In September 2009 a United Nations Fact Finding Mission issued a report setting out evidence that both sides had committed war crimes and other serious violations of international law. For example,

Israeli forces had carried out indiscriminate attacks against civilians, targeted and killed medical staff, used Palestinian civilians as human shields and fired white phosphorus over densely populated residential areas. More than 1,380 Palestinians, including over 330 children, were killed. Palestinian armed groups had indiscriminately launched rockets into Israeli population centres and 13 Israelis were killed.

Amnesty International campaigns for Israelis and Palestinians to live together in peace, prosperity and security, with their human rights and dignity respected and protected. We urge the Israeli authorities, Palestinian Authority and Palestinian armed groups to stop violating international humanitarian law and international human rights law. We campaign for justice and accountability for the long-suffering people of the region.

Youth groups

Amnesty International has an active membership of over 550 youth groups in the UK. Youth groups are gatherings of young people in schools, sixth-form colleges or youth clubs who meet to campaign for Amnesty. They hold publicity stunts, write letters to government leaders and officials, fundraise, get publicity in their local paper, hold assemblies and create displays. You can also join as an individual member and receive magazines and letter-writing actions.

If you would like to join Amnesty International, join or set up a youth group, or simply find out more, go to www.amnesty.org.uk/youth

Amnesty International UK, The Human Rights Action Centre
17–25 New Inn Yard, London EC2A 3EA   020 7033 1596
student@amnesty.org.uk
www.amnesty.org.uk

"It was 8.30 p.m. on 14 January; the area was quiet except of course there was always the noise of F-16s, Apaches, drones. There was no electricity. All my family were in the yard or the house listening to the news – negotiations in Egypt, martyrs, etc. The missile hit. Four were dead at once; my brother's body was all in pieces. We want to understand something: why did they hit our house? It is in a residential area. We are neither Hamas nor Fatah. We are all civilians. None of us did anything. My father was opposed to firing rockets against the Israelis; he wanted peace, and they killed him. We have nothing to do with the resistance. We don't understand. We want peace, and we want an investigation; we want to know why my sisters and I have been orphaned. Why did they kill our parents, our family? What life will we have now? Who will take care of us?"

Fathiya Mousa speaking to Amnesty International
(Fathiya's parents and siblings were killed in an Israeli air strike during Operation Cast Lead in January 2010.)

"My five-year-old son always asks where the closest bomb shelter is. Little children shouldn't have such worries; they should worry about what to play next."

Geut Aragon (Geut's house in Sderot, Israel, was hit by a Palestinian rocket in January 2009.)

jane mitchell

CHALKLINE

THE FINE LINE
BETWEEN BOY

AND SOLDIER

Rafiq's turn came and he stepped up to the chalk line. It reached the top of his ear. "This one is big enough. He goes in the truck. He's our first."

Rafiq is only nine when Kashmiri Freedom Fighters raid his village in search of new recruits. Tall for his age, he is the first boy to cross the chalk line into a life of brutality and violence.

Jameela cannot forget her brother. While Rafiq is trained to kill in the rebel camp high in the mountains, she keeps his memory alive.

When finally their paths cross again, Rafiq is unrecognizable as the boy who left the village. Will Jameela know him?

Endorsed by Amnesty International

PATRICIA McCORMICK

SOLD

CAN SHE EVER BE FREE?

Life is harsh in the mountain village in Nepal where Lakshmi works hard alongside her mother to look after the family. When her step-father finds her a job as a maid in the city, Lakshmi begins the long journey to India dreaming of earning money and making her family proud.

The truth that awaits her is a living nightmare.

"An unforgettable account of sexual slavery as it exists now." *Booklist*

US National Book Award finalist

Endorsed by Amnesty International

Gabriella Ambrosio is an Italian journalist and copywriter, a former professor and currently president of an international advertising agency in Italy. She has written several successful essays and recently contributed to *Freedom*, a short-story anthology celebrating the Universal Declaration of Human Rights, but *Before We Say Goodbye* (first published in Italy as *Prima di Lasciarsi*) is her first novel. It won an Italian first novel award at the Festival du Premier Romance in Chambery, France and is now also available in both Arabic and Hebrew. Gabriella lives with her husband and two children in Rome.

After working at a variety of jobs, **Alastair McEwen** spent ten years teaching English and history in Italy before finally turning to translation. Over the last 25 years he has translated over 70 books, including novels and non-fiction as well as essays, articles, poems, feature-film scripts and operatic librettos. Alastair has worked with many of Italy's finest living writers, including Roberto Calasso and Umberto Eco. He lives and works in Milan.